'Nobody is s ... bout Mr Williams' writ ... b:l:...
He has charm, ... has an authentic light touch, he understands
people, and his outlook on life is sophisticated'
*New York Times*

'Treasure is a likable suave hero'
*Booklist*

'His sense of character is as keen as his sense of place'
*Financial Times*

'Anyone who regrets the passing of the old-fashioned
detective story could do much worse than turn to Mr Williams,
with his astute but wry characterisation of English social life
and his adept plotting'
*Sunday Telegraph*

'Lots of hilarious touches'
*Guardian*

'Williams maintains suspense while keeping the masks of
comedy and tragedy spinning like tops'
*Sunday Times*

# MURDER IN ADVENT

Stuart David Williams was a writer best known for his crime novel series featuring the banker Mark Treasure and police inspector DI Parry.

After serving as Naval officer in WWII, Williams completed a History degree at St Johns College, Oxford, before embarking on a career in advertising. He became a full time fiction writer in 1978.

Williams wrote twenty-three novels, seventeen of which were part of the Mark Treasure series of whodunnits which began with *Unholy Writ* (1976). His experience in both the Anglican Church and the advertising world informed and inspired his work throughout his career.

Two of Williams' books were shortlisted for the Crime Writers' Association Gold Dagger Award, and in 1988 he was elected to the Detection Club.

*David Williams*

# MURDER IN ADVENT

PAN BOOKS

First published 1985 by Macmillan

This edition published 2016 by Pan Books
an imprint of Pan Macmillan
20 New Wharf Road, London N1 9RR
Associated companies throughout the world
www.panmacmillan.com

ISBN 978-1-5098-1538-8

1 3 5 7 9 8 6 4 2

A CIP catalogue record for this book is available from the British Library.

Typeset by Ellipsis Digital Limited, Glasgow
Printed and bound by CPI Group (UK) Ltd, Croydon, CR0 4YY

Visit www.panmacmillan.com to read more about all our books
and to buy them. You will also find features, author interviews and
news of any author events, and you can sign up for e-newsletters
so that you're always first to hear about our new releases.

*This one for*
*Michael and Elizabeth Sieff*

# Foreword

Three thousand miles across the Atlantic from England, at a big isolated house on the Florida coast, a skeletal male figure shuffles out of the elevator in the basement.

He is old, this lean, parched figure, tall and stooping, and dressed in a thin, ill-fitting light grey suit that flaps about him like a shroud. He crosses the carpeted corridor and operates the electric combination lock on the steel door opposite.

When the door slides open the man goes through into the wide, silent and carefully lit square gallery beyond. He closes the door again with a push button on the far side. It is cooler down here – the temperature kept at an unvarying level at all times to protect the exhibits. It is the same with the larger collection upstairs on the second floor, but the items here are in all senses even better protected.

The man sighs. The steely eyes wear a look of lustful anticipation. It is an expression that nowadays is more or less reserved for the daily visit to what most outsiders understand is a fall-out shelter.

He pauses with a sort of reverence before the Rembrandt Self-Portrait. Next his gaze devours the Corot Girl Musing by a Fountain – an especial favourite. Later he pays a kind of obeisance to the Rubens Christ on the Cross, and then caresses the fifteenth-century bas-relief Jesse's Tree because he finds its tactile quality a truly sensuous experience. When he comes to it, he stares very hard at his early Magna Carta, frowning as he remembers the promised report still hasn't been delivered. Breathing more heavily he moves on. The anger that has been welling in him is quickly dissipated at the sight of his *Van Dyck* Portrait of a High-Born Lady.

There are thirty-one exhibits altogether – not a large collection, but every one has, in its time, been something the man has desired and been temporarily denied. Some had not been for sale: others had been available only at exorbitant prices. The man is immensely rich as well as powerful, but he is not a fool with money. He had paid a proper price for every item – in an unconventional way. Each had come to him through the same special dealer. It is no inconvenience to him that the collection cannot be shown to others: on the contrary, as time goes by he draws increasing satisfaction from having to keep it all to himself. He has made arrangements for its disposal after his death – an event he considers is still a long way off. He is a widower recluse. Only his business manager and one trusted servant know of what is here.

Among his special favourite, the *Corot* had come from Montreal, the *Rubens* from Rome, the bas-relief from France, the *Rembrandt* and the *Van Dyck* from Italy and the *Magna Carta* from England: not all the items have been publicly reported as stolen – but the man knows they have been all the same.

# Chapter One

'*The Lord be with you,*' chanted Minor Canon Twist on B flat, unaccompanied and perfectly pitched. He allowed the last vowel to linger, then to dissolve in a refined diminuendo. The effect was nearly as pleasing to his hearers – and possibly even to God – as it was to Minor Canon Twist himself.

'*Aa-wey-wa-spey-wi-T,*' responded the choir of Litchester Cathedral in mellifluous, unisoned Donald Duck. The emphatic end consonant was marvellously arrested by the baffle that abruptly silences end consonants in cathedrals. This has something to do with tall, enclosed choir-stalls – but more with the way cathedral choir-masters fixate on emphatic end consonants.

The blind Dean Gilbert Hitt shifted his knees on his hassock. He was a big man: a sixty-two-year-old greyed eminence with an urbane wit and a reputation as a preacher. He had just read the second lesson. Processing to and from the lectern had warmed him a little, but the effect was fading. Every year they decreased the winter temperature in the cathedral by a degree. Not for the first time in early December the Dean took comfort that he'd likely be retired before the congregation was reduced to doing warming-up exercises in the stalls.

'*Lord, have mercy upon us,*' cantored Gerard Twist, who at twenty-eight, the dean calculated wryly, might survive to hear this standard supplication acquire an added poignancy.

'*Chri-aa-aa-see-aa-aw-u-Su,*' cawed the choir at a congregation which it comfortably outnumbered, and all of whose members understood the chanted words without benefit of translation. There were fifteen such worshippers spread out along the canopied back rows of intricately carved canons' stalls on both sides of the chancel aisle. The officiating clergy sat here too, in the end seats nearest the nave. Next to the Dean was gaunt, bearded Canon Brastow, the Cathedral Treasurer. Immediately opposite on the right-hand side was the ample Canon Merit, the Chancellor and thus second in the Chapter pecking order. Between him and Minor Canon Twist knelt the impish and ebullient Canon Ewart Jones, Precentor. In front, in paired rows of stalls, were the robed choristers.

All week-day services were held in the enclosed choir – the part of the chancel immediately east of the crossing of the nave with the north and south transepts, and the massive central tower that marked that crossing and illuminated it with its Norman lantern.

Litchester Cathedral is almost wholly Norman, where rounded arch everywhere imposes over rounded arch, where there is solidity in immense pillars, magnificence in breadth as well as in height, majesty in length, the whole structure breathtakingly awesome – and ruinously expensive to run.

The diocese is small – like the town which, despite its having a cathedral, is seldom now referred to as a city. Litchester is smaller than neighbouring Hereford and Shrewsbury, or more distant Worcester and Gloucester. Only its cathedral is bigger – and poorer too, than any of those others. It is also less visited because it is less accessible, and despite its being indisputably one of the finest examples of Romanesque architecture in Europe.

The cathedral choir is not outstanding. Years ago it had been. Now there isn't the money. The choir school still exists – just, but it's generally known it will have to go in the next lot of cuts. Meantime all the boys are recruited from the town: boarding facilities were abolished some years ago. Girls and young women are now admitted to the choir. There had been trouble about that from traditionalists, but the singing had improved. None of the choir men – the clerks choral – is full-time. Most work in banks or building society branches in the town. It's why the week-day sung evensong is held as late as five o'clock. Of course, with an extra million pounds in the funds . . .

'*O Lord, save Thy people,*' beseeched Twist.

'*And bless Thine inheritance,*' Canon Brastow, tall and ascetic, responded reedily and unexpectedly from beside the Dean, interrupting the latter's retrospections – and half a beat ahead of the choir's appointed response.

The Dean sighed to himself: Clive Brastow was testing his voice in preparation for leading the spoken prayers after the anthem. He had earlier complained of a sore throat. He was Canon Residentiary during December, which presaged a succession of Sunday sermons on social responsibility, the misconduct of the rich, and prescriptions for Third World ills. These would come at a time when Dean Hitt considered people could be better employed having their hearts and minds prepared for the joys of Christmas.

At least Brastow had declared himself in favour of selling the exemplification: the Dean was steering his own mind to more charitable postulations. But was the fellow going to insist on those conditions? The priorities were absolutely clear without tomfool qualifications from members of the Chapter.

If only dear Ewart Jones would see sense.

'*Lighten our darkness, we beseech Thee, O Lord . . .*'

Gerard Twist's chanting of the third collect was too evidently a sensitively modulated solo to command attention as mere prayer. The over-prompt, identifiable 'Amen' at the end, emanating in a good, clear contralto from further down the Dean's row, came more as a musical appreciation than a pious affirmation. That would be Laura Purse, an engaging spinster of this cathedral, and its librarian-archivist. It was the same attractive Miss Purse whose intentions concerning Minor Canon Twist had for some time been clearer to most present than they had seemed to have been to the Minor Canon himself.

The anthem that came next was a modern piece which the Dean didn't much care for – so his renewed resolve to apply his mind wholly to the service fell by the wayside once again. He knelt with everyone else when the choir stopped singing. Canon Brastow launched into prayers for the royal family with an almost treasonable lack of spirit and a voice only just made audible through the microphone in front of him.

The Dean returned to pondering on Canon Ewart Jones after consciously determining the Queen could manage without his personal intercession till the morrow.

Ewart's stand about the sale of the exemplification was the more irritating for being infuriatingly explicable. He and the Dean were friends. Both men had been nurtured in the High Church tradition. Both were informed if uncomplicated believers. Both instinctively rejected the trendy, modernist disbeliefs. Both were family men, and both were conservatives – the Dean by instinct, the Canon by experience. The high-born Oxford classicist and the New Zealand farmworker's outstanding son rarely had difficulty in reaching accord. They'd have had none now over the selling of the Litchester Magna Carta if the Dean's view had matched the attitudes and values to which the two men normally subscribed. The Dean accepted that he was the inconsistent party. But he still felt his stand was more than justified.

'. . . and dost promise, that when two or three are gathered together . . .' Brastow was making husky going of the prayer of St Chrysostom. Canon Merit had earlier read the first lesson for him after volunteering to do so – and the prayers as well if he wanted – when Brastow had complained about his throat in the vestry.

Almost anything Merit offered to do for Brastow – or Brastow for Merit – would be accepted grudgingly because it could be logged by the donor as a conciliatory gesture. They were not friends. It would be uncharitable to say they were enemies – just some distance apart on theological, doctrinal, liturgical, political, and social issues, which, it's true, left very few others on which they could be at all close.

If Canon Jones, the Precentor, had offered to take over the whole of the Canon Residentiary's bits of the service – which he very nearly did, except Merit got in first – the offer would have been accepted with alacrity. As it was, Brastow had only himself and his pride to blame that while capitulating over the reading of the first lesson he was still left struggling with the prayers. As he made his way through them painfully, he avoided glancing across the aisle for fear of catching what he was sure would be Merit's over-solicitous look signalling that he could still take over.

It was unusual for all four members of the cathedral's governing body – the Dean, the Chancellor, the Treasurer and the Precentor – to be together at a Thursday evensong. They were present this time because Dean Hitt had summoned a special Chapter meeting just before. At times there had been acrimony at the meeting. By common but unspoken charitable intention they had all come on to the service directly from the Chapter House.

'*Fulfil now, O Lord, the desires and petitions of Thy servants . . .*' Brastow soldiered on, smoothing his beard on to his afflicted throat.

Canon Algy Merit, extreme Anglo-Catholic, and New Testament scholar, fifty-two-year-old bachelor aesthete and portly gourmet, dropped his gaze and gave up trying to attract Brastow's attention. Now he bent his head half to one side, and in this characteristic pose appeared to be studying the upper buttons of his cassock. The folds under his chin sank well into his neck. His pink and shining cheeks sagged also in repose.

If Brastow found croaking preferable to applying common sense, so be it, judged the Chancellor to himself. He was still finding it difficult to understand quite why the Dean had drawn such comfort from the Treasurer's attitude over the exemplification. The condition Brastow was attaching to his approval of a sale wholly nullified the value from the cathedral's viewpoint.

Merit's brow wrinkled as he closed his eyelids. His own attitude had been unequivocal: honest and unequivocal. He would consent to selling if a guaranteed British buyer could be found. Under no circumstances would he co-operate over the present offer. The eyelids tightened. It was a matter of principle. So, an early thirteenth century exemplification of the Magna Carta was not strictly a work of art: facing facts – it wasn't a work of art at all. The left cheek twitched. Nevertheless, you couldn't be the author of a quite recent letter to *The Times* deploring the sale and export of irreplaceable treasures from British collections and then be party to flogging one yourself to a museum in California. He flicked the check with an extended forefinger.

Plenty of people would consider the Litchester Magna Carta as irreplaceable treasure. Of course, there was no British buyer – nor would there be at more than a million pounds, nor anything approaching it. Canon Merit opened his eyes to watch as well as hear Brastow trying to stifle a nasty cough.

'. . . *and in the world to come, life everlasting.*'

'Amen,' responded Lieutenant-Commander Bliter, RN (Retired), five seats along from Merit, and admiring the way Canon Brastow was coping under handicap.

Percival Arbuthnot Bliter was the Cathedral Administrator. He normally stopped work at four and wasn't a regular attendant at evensong. Today was different. He had been formally required to take the minutes at the Chapter meeting and, not to put too fine a point on it, attending the service afterwards had offered a nice earnest of his piety to virtually all those who held authority over him. He had come in late, but he hadn't been the last.

Bliter had retired from the Royal Navy six years earlier, at the age of forty-seven. The cathedral job didn't pay as much as he'd have liked, but it was suitable in the social sense, the hours were short, and after two years of unemployment he had been glad to take it – as well as the rent-free apartments in Abbot's Cloister. His service pension was indexed, which meant it kept pace with the general cost of living but not with the specific price of gin.

Percy Bliter had been a disappointment to his father, an admiral, also to his wife Jennifer, an admiral's daughter. He had even been a disappointment to himself, but he didn't let failure show, priding himself on maintaining standards, albeit ones that in the material context the Bliters had never at any time attained. There had been no children.

Slowly he turned his head altarwise, making the movement seem like an act of devotion. He stole a lascivious glance at Cindy Larks in the choir opposite, before his gaze came to rest on Miles Nutkin, the Chapter Clerk, in the seat beside him and whose eyes he guessed would be closed. Percy deferred to Nutkin, who had appointed him to his job in the first place.

The Administrator straightened his back and the knot of his Royal Navy tie. He was a tall and commanding figure, even when kneeling – and a bluff, jolly Jack Tar of a chap was another of the impressions he liked to foster. He sometimes prayed, and he did so now in his own way.

'God, make them sell the Magna Carta' was the simple sailor's heartfelt, silent entreaty.

As if on cue, Nutkin's eyes flickered open and stared momentarily at Bliter, who started guiltily. It was well known the Chapter Clerk was against the sale – but not that he could intercept messages to the Almighty.

'Hymn number six,' announced Minor Canon Twist.

Miles Nutkin had been at the Chapter meeting in an advisory capacity. He, too, had felt obliged to attend the service. He had come in well after the start but he had needed to make some telephone calls: also he had run into Mrs Hitt, the Dean's wife.

The title of Chapter Clerk was a formal one, at once more important though less onerous than it sounded. The office was part-time and rewarded with an honorarium. The holder was required to be a practising solicitor, to be an adviser to the Dean and Chapter – mostly on matters of law – when occasion arose, and to appear at special services and functions clad in official regalia.

Nutkin, though a year younger than Bliter, looked much the senior of the two. He was of medium height, slight build, and balding at the front, which served to accentuate a wide, high forehead. The thick spectacles with the heavy frames added to the general gravity of his appearance: so did his dark suits. He frowned a good deal and seldom smiled. He was married, and as well as being an important lawyer – the principal of a long-established family practice – he was a county councillor, on the board of the Litchester Building Society, inconspicuously rich, and preparing to become even richer. He was considered a prayerful and thoughtful man. In the previous half-hour he had prayed very little but had certainly been thinking hard. Seldom had the Dean and Chapter given him so much to think about.

> 'He comes the broken heart to bind
> The bleeding soul to cure
> And with the treasures of his grace
> To enrich the humble poor.'

Canon Jones, the breezy New Zealander, had as good a voice as any of the clerks choral: bass baritone, well controlled. He savoured the third verse of 'Hark the Glad Sound' and smiled up broadly and a touch mischievously at Algy Merit, while providing a spirited rendering to the last two lines.

In the organ loft, above and behind the north choir-stalls, Dr Donald Welt, cathedral organist, opened more stops before crashing into the last verse of the hymn. Misgiving accompanied his action since he never knew how much fortissimo the instrument would take. Ninety-eight thousand pounds was the estimate for the urgent organ restoration work. And the fools down there were actually debating whether to sell their lousy Magna Carta.

The short brawny musician threw back his head, dark eyes glinting angrily, the full beard below the shock of wiry black hair adding to the Mephistophelian visage. The arms and legs thrashed at the keyboards and pedals in a way that might have defied accuracy. But the sound was magnificent – like the talents of the player, which, people grudgingly agreed, went some way to balance the uncomfortable suspicion that the organist was not only a lecher but also an agnostic lecher.

As Welt had struck that opening chord, Mr Pounder, the Dean's verger, had been conducting the blind Gilbert Hitt to the steps of the high altar ready to give the blessing. Pounder moved to the side, a frail, gaunt figure in his black robe and dark suit. He was a very old man: no one seemed to know quite how old. His head was bowed and trembled a little from time to time. His face, as always, bore an expression of benign contentment.

The heavy silver, lead-filled mace was tucked into the crook of his left arm.

Mr Pounder was not allowed into Chapter meetings, of course, but he knew well enough what the business had been at the meeting today. You could hardly be involved with the cathedral and not know.

It was a bad business in Mr Pounder's view, and not one over which he found it easy to understand the Dean's attitude – not that he would admit as much to anyone save the Dean, who hadn't asked him and wasn't likely to. But Mr Pounder had long let it be known he owned an affection for the Litchester Magna Carta that exceeded his regard for all other inanimate objects – and many animate ones, not excluding some human beings. He'd go any distance to stop that parchment falling into unworthy hands, and he advised that others should be minded to do the same.

As a lad he'd bought a copy of the wording – not the words on the Magna Carta: they were in Latin. A translation was what he'd got and roughly memorised. King John had put his hand to those words in a meadow called Runnymede. *First, that we have granted to God that the English Church shall be free and its liberties unimpaired.* And so they were still.

Mr Pounder glanced approvingly at the assembled adults and children exercising their common right if varying capacities freely to make worshipful glad sounds in the chancel below him – and in the oldest part of the building. The choir and nave were said to have been finished a hundred years before the Magna Carta.

*To all free men of our kingdom we have also granted, for us and our heirs for ever, all the liberties here set out.* And the liberties written down had been the same ones he'd gone to defend when he'd volunteered for the Army.

He'd been in his late thirties already when the last war started, but he'd been marching behind the colours from the first day – to defend the freedoms he'd seen set out in Magna Carta.

Mr Pounder's head shook more vigorously, and this time in a quite controlled sort of way. You couldn't buy freedom with money – and you shouldn't try selling it to the highest bidder, either. That was why he felt the guilt of the thing so badly. To him, selling the Litchester Magna Carta was the same as putting your freedom in jeopardy – and your self-respect. He'd been insisting on that with more justification than people knew. It had got to the point where he found it hard to live with what was happening.

'. . . *and the fellowship of the Holy Ghost, be with you all evermore.*' The Dean ended without being aware that, for the first time in his verger's lifetime involvement with the cathedral, Mr Pounder had been so preoccupied with his thoughts he'd omitted to kneel for the blessing.

One of the younger girl choristers noticed the lapse. She was to remark next day that Mr Pounder had become forgetful, being so old.

'He couldn't have meant any disrespect,' she went on. 'Be awful if he had, wouldn't it? Him being dead within the hour.'

'*Aa-aa-aa-aa-aaa-me-Nu.*' The choir had sung a long, harmonious valediction.

# Chapter Two

'"Exemplification" being the posh word for "copy", of course,' said Mark Treasure into the telephone. The forty-four-year-old merchant banker was seated in his elegantly appointed office at Grenwood, Phipps in the City of London.

'Actually an attested copy, Mr Treasure,' the young woman at the other end replied promptly. 'In this case, very much attested. You know the one you're interested in has King Henry III's seal on it? Not King John's.' Fiona Gore jammed the receiver between her aristocratic ear and shapely shoulder while both hands scrabbled amongst the litter of documents on the table in front of her. Her shared office at Christie's, the world-famous auctioneers in King Street, St James's, was fairly Spartan, its only really elegant appointment being Fiona.

Treasure knew about the seal. 'And there are three other copies of the 1225 version of Magna Carta?'

'Three for certain. One in the British Museum. One at Durham Cathedral. The other's in the Public Record Office in Chancery Lane.'

'All hugely prized. Curious since King John signed the original Magna Carta in 1215. You'd have thought . . .'

'Sealed it.'

'I'm sorry?'

'He didn't sign it, Mr Treasure.'

'You're quite right, Fiona. I'd forgotten.'

She smiled to herself. She hadn't spent the whole day boning up on Magna Carta in all its aspects to trip over the most celebrated if trivial misconception in British history. 'Were you going to say it's odd that the 1225 copies are so valuable? That copies of the 1215, the first version, ought to be even more so?'

'That's exactly what I intended . . .'

'Well, they are. More valuable. Or potentially so. Except there's never been one put to sale. Nor likely to be. So it's rather academic. Anyway, there are only four of those surviving, too.'

'Only four of the 1215 version?'

'That's out of thirteen we know were made. Two of the copies are in the British Library. Lincoln and Salisbury Cathedrals have the others.'

'Four of each surviving after nearly eight centuries. Not bad, I suppose. On the other hand, it's difficult to credit why any of them should've been destroyed. Knowingly destroyed.'

'Lots of things like that disappeared during the dissolution of the monasteries. Under Henry VIII. And they're not that big.'

'Easily filched?'

'Or mislaid.' Fiona clearly took a less jaundiced view of human nature than Treasure. 'Yours only measures twelve inches by seventeen. That's not including the seal. And Magna Carta wasn't always revered. For a time you were cursed if you looked at one. When the Pope disapproved.'

'That would reduce the keeping qualities, certainly.'

'Anyway, it's why the four copies of the 1225 Charter are still relatively valuable.'

'Wasn't the thing rewritten in 1216 as well?'

'Reissued after King John's death in that year. And again in 1217. Durham Cathedral has the only copy of the first. The Bodleian Library, Oxford, has the only copy of the second.'

'They weren't important?'

'Depends on what you consider important, Mr Treasure. All the reissues had alterations and amendments.'

'The 1225 more than the others?'

'Mm. It was called the Great Reissue.'

'Consolidated the alterations in the others, perhaps?'

'That's about it. They went on making reissues through the thirteenth century. Through the reigns of Henry III and Edward I.

Till the Final Great Reissue in October 1297. Funny, there are four of those surviving, too. That version became Statute Law.'

'Enshrined in our national heritage. Protecting the freedom of every citizen.' Treasure was musing more than declaiming.

Fiona giggled. 'Only freemen and upwards got their rights protected. Most people at the time were bondsmen and serfs. They weren't covered by Magna Carta. And things didn't alter much during the century.'

'Did you say more copies of the 1225 reissue were distributed?'

'According to Matthew Paris, contemporary chronicler, copies went to every county.'

'How many would that be?'

Fiona frowned. 'Doesn't say in the commentary I'm reading from. More than fifty, I should think.'

Treasure was drawing circles around some of the figures he'd written on the pad in front of him. 'Four seems to be a popular number for surviving copies of important issues.'

'Because there are four each of the 1215, the 1225 and the 1297? That's coincidence, of course. I'll have more on the location of lesser versions tomorrow. From the British Library. The Assistant Keeper's been terribly helpful.'

'I'm grateful. What a beaver you are. But I shan't be here tomorrow. If you wouldn't mind talking to my secretary, Miss Gaunt.'

'Or Peregrine if she's busy?' Fiona was giggling again. Treasure knew her through her brother Peregrine, who worked at the bank.

Although the Grenwood, Phipps research department was resourceful in most ways, it was evidently not geared for fast devilling into the provenance of ancient documents – even when the enquiry came from the bank's Vice-Chairman and Chief Executive. It had been briefed the day before on Treasure's requirements and had yet to come back with its answers. Fiona had been briefed in the same hour – at Miss Gaunt's suggestions.

'Your brother may not want to be troubled. He's involved in a flotation we're doing. And, talking of big money, d'you have the answer to my burning question?'

'About the value of your 1225 exemplification? That can't wait?'

'No. So give me an intelligent guess. You've done spectacularly well in every other way.'

'Thank you. We aim to please. And you are a respected Christie customer. It's only that my boss would have done much better than me. He's a walking encyclopaedia on medieval manuscripts. He'll be back next week.'

'Too late for my purpose. You don't feel you should chance your arm?'

'It's not exactly that. There are loads of imponderables involved.'

'Such as?'

'Whether the Government might try to stop the issue of an export licence. You said the offer's from America.'

'I think the Government would have trouble if it tried to block the sale. It's not a picture. The thing isn't unique. It's not nearly so well known as the 1215 version at Salisbury, for instance. Nor apparently so well protected.'

'It's a significant historical object, even so. Emotions might be stirred.'

'Lot of repairs needed at Litchester Cathedral, too,' the banker countered pointedly.

'A picture would certainly be different.' Fiona was hedging. 'There are precedents with important pictures. At auction we might know who'd be making the serious bidding. Roughly the minimum price we could expect.'

'In this case there's one firm buyer knocking down the door. Private sale. No auctioneer's costs.'

'Shame on you, Mr Treasure. Obviously means your buyer's a nutter for Magna Cartas. May also be the only one. In which case . . .'

'We should grab his money and run?'

'Depends how much money. And you're still not going to tell me?'

'Might prejudice your judgement.'

She hesitated for a moment. 'OK. I feel unless the offer's for over a million pounds you'd be better going to auction.'

'Ah. So if you had it to auction you'd put a reserve of a million on it?'

'That or a shade under, perhaps. And it doesn't mean we'd guarantee to get the reserve, of course. It's just if you had to sell it for less than a million I think you might come to regret it.'

'Fiona, I'm enormously grateful. You should join the bank. You're even brainier than your brother.'

'Younger, too.'

'And a hell of a lot prettier.'

'Flattery will get you absolutely anywhere, Mr Treasure,' she answered, meaning it.

Treasure was still smiling to himself after replacing the receiver, and was mildly disconcerted when he looked up to see Lord Grenwood hovering in the open doorway.

'Am I interrupting, Mark?' The elderly non-executive Chairman of the bank advanced into the room beaming – head and neck leant backwards, arms held still at the sides but bent upwards at the elbows. Not much of the gnomish Lord Grenwood seemed to articulate below the knee-joints as he padded purposefully to one of the chairs in front of Treasure's desk.

'Glad to see you, Bertie. Need your opinion.' Treasure looked at the time. It was five-fifteen. 'Late for you, isn't it?'

'Sherry party at the Mansion House. With the Lord Mayor. One feels obliged. Shan't stay long.' Normally Lord Grenwood went home before the rush hour – after arriving at the bank in time for lunch. He was well past retirement age. Coming to the City every day gave him a purpose in life – and pleased his wife. 'Miss Gaunt says you're not going to Milan.'

'Meeting cancelled. Going to Litchester instead.'

'Litchester? Litchester? I seem to remember . . .'

'The vicar's warden of Great St Agnes Church across the road has a connection with the cathedral there.' Since total enlightenment had yet to be reflected on the older man's face, Treasure continued. 'There's an expensive copy of the Magna Carta at the cathedral. Given to the Dean and Chapter in 1694 by a wealthy London wool merchant called Edwards. Later Alderman Edwards. Actually he gave it collectively to them and the vicar's warden of Great St Agnes.' Now he picked up a letter and read from it. ' "To be kept, maintained, or disposed of in their absolute discretion, and if there be any dispute the same to be resolved by a simple majority of them all, duly summoned and assembled." ' Treasure looked up at Lord Grenwood. 'Were you ever duly summoned to Litchester?'

'Certainly not. Been there, of course. Difficult place to get to. Practically in mid-Wales. On the border anyway.' He shook his head to indicate things could hardly be worse than that. Then as an afterthought came: 'I do remember I was at one time . . .'

'Vicar's warden at Great St Agnes,' Treasure cut in. 'So was your father, and your grandfather. Nowadays it's me, pressed into service by you and the vicar when you gave it up.' Grenwood, Phipps made large and regular contributions to the church's up-keep. 'In 1694 Alderman Edwards, the benefactor, was vicar's warden. He was born in Litchester.'

'And that's why you're going there?' Grenwood nodded at his own perspicacity.

'Because there's a dispute about selling the Magna Carta. Has to be resolved tomorrow.'

'You can sell church property without a by-your-leave?'

'This isn't church property. It was very specifically given to the Litchester Dean and Chapter. And to me.' Treasure grinned and continued: 'Alderman Edwards apparently feared a Jacobite revival, leading to sequestration of English church property by the Pope of Rome. He was a staunch Orangeman.'

'So who's disputing what?'

'The Dean and Chapter. That's the Dean and the three canons. Two are for selling. Two against. The Dean being for. They've been that way for some time. The Dean's called a formal meeting of all parties for tomorrow.'

'Which includes you?'

'Yes. I'd intended to send my excuses. And my view, naturally, when I'd formed one. Not sure that would have counted as a vote. But now the Italian trip's cancelled.' He shrugged.

'You feel it's a sign?'

'In a way. That I ought to observe a clear obligation if I can.'

'Molly still in California?'

'Mm. Filming for another three weeks.' They were talking of Treasure's actress wife. 'Oh, I can quite easily get away. Problem's been deciding which way to vote. Whether the thing should be sold and, if so, for how much.'

'And you'll have the casting vote?'

'Precisely. Nutkin, the Chapter Clerk, rang me at lunchtime. They were having another Chapter meeting this afternoon, a final attempt to resolve things without me. He'd sent me formal notice of tomorrow's meeting some time ago.' He indicated the letter on his desk again.

Lord Grenwood shifted in his chair. 'Bit embarrassing for them, having the decision depend on an outsider. Awkward. They didn't settle it this afternoon?' He shook his head as if he knew the answer.

'No. Nutkin rang me again just now to say they were very much counting on my being there in the morning.'

'And how shall you vote?'

'It's why I wanted your view. How would you have voted?'

The old man stopped digging a finger into his right ear, and adopted an especially solemn expression. He remained silent for several moments, breathing heavily. 'No idea,' he said eventually and in the way of someone who had ceased to be ashamed of ducking responsibility. 'Anyone lobbied you?'

'Not really.' There had been a letter he thought too trivial to mention. 'I've only spoken with Nutkin.'

The other looked perplexed, as though this witness to ecclesiastical probity surprised him. 'Pity to sell assets of that kind. If it's not necessary. Bound to go on appreciating. Scarcity value, don't you know?'

'That's what I told Nutkin when he was first in touch. Now I believe I've changed my mind. Told him that, too. Thought it only fair.' Treasure paused. 'It's a totally unproductive asset. Earns nothing and must cost a lot in insurance. It's not sacred. Nor a work of art. And the cathedral's desperate for money.'

'How much will it fetch?'

'Christie's suggest over a million.'

'God bless my soul,' expostulated Lord Grenwood in awe at the sum and not in hope of celestial preferment for elderly merchant bankers.

'And £1.1 million has already been offered. By a Californian museum. Offer's been on the table for six months. It's being withdrawn at midday tomorrow if it's not accepted and the Magna Carta lodged with a local bank.'

Grenwood stiffened. 'Sounds pretty cavalier.'

'Not really. Buyer's fed up with vacillation. He's put half a million on call as immediate part-payment, the remainder of the purchase price in seven days. That's after formal proving of the document. It's all a ploy to concentrate our minds, of course. Succeeded, too.'

'Christie's know all this?'

'No. Not the amount of the offer. That's confidential to Chapter members.'

'Money's good, I suppose? American buyer, you say?' Lord Grenwood had been pursuing his banking apprenticeship in New York at the time of the Wall Street crash. Subsequently he had never quite developed what might be termed an unswerving sense of reliance on American financial institutions. 'Californian bank?' he added narrowly. 'Which one?'

'A good one, Bertie. And the money's there all right. But is it enough? On balance I think it is.' Treasure blew a pout. 'It's why I've come around to selling. And selling tomorrow.'

'Without risking an auction.' His Lordship's right hand absently searched the top of his head for strands of hair that hadn't been there for years. 'That's wise if no one else is showing interest.'

'And no one is. Not currently. There was a potential buyer nearly four years ago. Also American, but not the same one. Made an offer of four hundred thousand pounds. The Dean and Chapter turned it down. Unanimously.'

'You weren't involved?'

'Wasn't necessary. Except the Chapter Clerk wrote at the time to say what happened. Out of courtesy.'

'So there could be another buyer there?'

'I asked Nutkin. He thinks not. Whoever it was acted through an agent. The agent's been contacted. Says his client's dead.'

Grenwood consulted his gold half-hunter watch. 'Well, glad to have been of help,' he pronounced confidently. 'Now I must go. You motoring to Litchester?'

'No. Train's quicker. Seven-twelve from Euston. Takes two hours. Has a diner.'

'Very sensible this time of year.' He stood up. 'Don't think I know the Dean of Litchester.'

'Gilbert Hitt? I've not met him either. Celebrated chap. Lost his sight as a child, in an accident.'

'And he's in favour of selling the Magna Carta.' Grenwood shook his head. 'I've always found old documents nice things to look upon. Except my birth certificate. Case of beauty being in the eye of the beholder, I suppose.'

'Not in the eye of Dean Hitt, of course.' Treasure also stood up.

'That's really what I meant.'

# Chapter Three

'You'll give it more thought, Ewart?' The Dean had his arm linked with Canon Jones's.

'You make it hard for me to think of anything else, Gilbert.' The New Zealand open 'a' made the word 'hard' seem harder still. The sentence had in any case been delivered with characteristic sharpness and energy.

The clergymen were leaving the cathedral after evensong by the main north door. This led to a wide, low, fan-vaulted porch open on three sides with another storey above. Mr Duggan, the head verger, watched them go with a bow more obsequious than ceremonious – and also purposeless since the Dean couldn't see it and the Precentor was preoccupied. The man's ingratiating smile changed to a worried look as soon as they were past, and as he set off at a brisk pace for the vergers' robing room murmuring to himself.

Outside it was dark and dry. A cold wind was sweeping through the cathedral close, scattering brittle leaves from the beech trees and swirling them around the copper-topped, old-fashioned lamp standards.

Litchester Cathedral stands in the centre of its own rectangular precinct. The area to the south is largely occupied by two adjoining quadrangles: Abbot's Cloister converted to house clergy and staff, and Bishop's Cloister which links with the Bishop's Palace standing below it on the banks of the River Litchin.

The wide, grassy close, dissected by broad walks, is set around the other three sides of the cathedral. The concrete walk the two were joining runs the length of the building: at its western end it broaches the middle of Bridge Street, while in the east it finishes at the gates into East Street below the Deanery. Another walk runs straight up from the porch to narrow North Street – now only a pedestrian way lined with small shops – and which in turn disgorges on to Market Square.

The Deanery occupies most of the upper east side of the close. The Precentor's house, where Canon Jones lives, is next door. Both buildings are Jacobean. In contrast, the Chancellor's and the Treasurer's houses are early Georgian. They were built as a pair in 1716 by a pupil of Wren's and stand to left and right of the opening to North Street. The New Chapter House dates from slightly later, and is in the north-west corner of the close, back to back with the modern post office in Bridge Street.

The two men turned east into the wind. They made an odd couple: the Dean a big, impressive figure in cloak over cassock, proceeded with dignity. Canon Jones, terrier-like, seemed more to be making a series of close-encounter lunges at his superior than to be acting as his guide. Only the fact of the linked arms prevented the small wiry Precentor from making wider sallies and generally more extravagant attempts at physical punctuation – demonstrations largely lost as emphatic ploys on a blind companion. Even so, his friend's erratic behaviour was the source of mild irritation to the other – and not for the first time.

'You're doing exercises round me again, Ewart.' The Dean interrupted something Canon Jones had been saying.

'Sorry.' The Precentor attempted to fall in with the other's stolid stride before continuing. 'What I've tried to explain is I couldn't square my conscience with posterity. Not over the sale. We're only tenants of this great property.' He waved his free arm in the direction of the cathedral. 'Courtesy of our predecessors. We owe it to them–'

'To see the place doesn't fall down.'

'To find new money to keep it all intact.'

'From where?'

'They found money. Every century produced its own extra

richness, Gilbert. They didn't sell the cathedral plate. They acquired it. Passed it on to us.'

'We're not selling the cathedral plate, either. Wouldn't dream of it.'

'Principle's the same.'

'Not at all. Magna Carta was a confidence trick.'

'To which we owe habeas corpus, not to mention trial by jury . . .'

'Only a colonial would believe that.'

'Franklin Roosevelt used to quote from Magna Carta.'

'Makes my point.'

'What point?'

'You're exercising again. I can make better progress on my own.' Which was true. In the cathedral and its precinct the Dean, aided by his folding white stick, was quite as good at directions as a sighted person. He made to drop the other's arm.

'Hang on, Gilbert.' The Precentor halted, which meant they both had to. 'I simply can't accept that the good people of this diocese won't find the money for the organ . . .'

'And the roof repairs, and the choir-school endowment, and an urgent increase in general income.'

'If £1.1 million will cover it . . .'

'It won't. But it'll be a start. Ask the Treasurer. And if you were Treasurer you wouldn't be so sanguine.'

It was the Precentor's traditional task to arrange the services, approve the music and generally to supervise worship. It was true that, unlike Canon Brastow, he wasn't responsible for the protection of cathedral property, nor, in a general way, for the balancing of its books. On the face of it, he was more involved in spending the cathedral's income than in raising it.

'I want the organ repaired more than Clive Brastow does.' Ewart Jones tapped the Dean lightly on the chest with an extended forefinger to help make his point. 'He's only in favour of selling the exemplification so the money can go to . . . to colonials,' he ended triumphantly, jabbing again, only harder. 'That's his condition.'

'He'll change it.'

'I doubt it.'

'So do I.'

'That's honest anyway. Gilbert, if we charged a pound admission to rubber-neckers it'd bring in an extra quarter million a year for starters.'

'Controversial.'

'They make an entrance charge at Salisbury Cathedral.'

'It's voluntary.'

'But you've got to be smart to get in without paying it. All right, so what about a straightforward cathedral appeal?'

'So what about selling the wretched Magna Carta?'

'Because it's too easy. Because it's selling out a trust. Because it'd be the opposite of the benefactor's intention.'

'Nonsense. He was simply opposed to Rome. We're not anti-Rome.'

'You think he'd have been in favour of Californian museums?'

'Difficult to tell. And we shan't find out standing here in the freezing cold while you pummel me in the solar plexus.' The Dean marched on independently at a brisk pace, opening his stick as he went. 'No doubt the vicar's warden of Great St Agnes will provide the resolution,' he concluded without enthusiasm.

'Ha! No doubt at all, according to Miles Nutkin.' Canon Jones, taken unawares, had to hurry to catch up. 'And full marks to a banker who isn't on the side of the asset-strippers.'

Except Canon Jones had not been brought up to date on Treasure's current attitude.

Canon Merit filled two glasses with a very dry sherry, and replaced the cut-glass decanter on the silver tray which stood on the side-table in his panelled study. He handed one of the glasses to the Chapter Clerk, then moved with the other to the small rack of reference books he kept on his desk.

'So Mr Treasure has changed his mind?' he said.

'Quite certainly, I'm afraid, Chancellor.' Miles Nutkin looked worried. As always on formal occasions, he was careful to use the

proper titles in addressing members of the cathedral's upper hierarchy. True, this was only a semi-formal occasion: Merit had
pressed him to drop in for a brief discussion after the service. Even
so, Nutkin knew one could never overdo the niceties with the
Chancellor.

Algy Merit was broadly responsible for cathedral legal and
educational matters. He was given to stressing that the Chancel-
lorship was not simply an important dignity – though it was
certainly that, too. He considered his exemplary performance in
the office tokened his suitability to be made Dean when Gilbert
Hitt retired – or else that it pointed him towards a more important
elevation in the wider sphere: everyone knew this. At fifty-two
promotion of some kind was beginning to look urgent for the
Chancellor: everyone knew this, too.

'It could suggest Mr Treasure may change his mind yet again,
of course,' Merit observed almost absently – though not convin-
cingly so. He was turning the pages of *Who's Who*, a volume his
detractors insisted he referred to more often than he did the Bible.

'Difficult to say. When I spoke to him on the telephone three
weeks ago he was as anxious as . . . as we are not to sell.' Nutkin
sucked in air through his nearly closed lips while watching for the
expression of approval to mark his confirming their common
cause: he got it in the quick lift of the eyebrows. Although the
Chapter Clerk had no vote in the making of Chapter decisions, he
behaved as though he had. 'When I rang him just before evensong,
he was taking a quite different stance. Very disquieting.' He
paused. 'If I'd seen this coming, I frankly wouldn't have pressed
him so hard – to attend the meeting tomorrow.'

'This doesn't tell us much. Quite a short entry.' Since people
listed in *Who's Who* are required to write their own entries Algy
Merit was invariably surprised to come upon a brief one: his
own was substantial. 'Aged forty-four. Married. Educated Jesus
College, Oxford. Banker all his life. Ah, Chairman of the Anglican Cathedrals' Protection Trust. Protection ought to equate with
maintaining the status quo. Doesn't always, of course.'

Canon Merit closed and replaced the book, then joined his

visitor before the log fire. He adjusted the purple-edged shoulder-cape he was wearing over his cassock. There was nothing to say he was entitled to purple edging: equally, there was nothing to say he wasn't – or so he had been advised by a fashionable ecclesiastical outfitter. He also had purple-covered buttons on his best cassock – the silk one. He took a large draught of the sherry, rolling it around his mouth before swallowing it. 'And he arrives tonight, you say?'

'Treasure? Yes. Staying at the Red Dragon.'

'We might have put him up here. Could have seemed – like an attempt at influence, I suppose. People are sometimes given to assume motives on the flimsiest of grounds.' They both knew he meant Canon Brastow. 'You'll agree, Miles, I've made it quite plain where my objections lie?'

'Absolutely.'

'I am not averse to selling the exemplification – at the right price. I simply can't sanction its being sold to go abroad.'

'No likelihood of a British buyer at that price, of course. The Treasurer . . .'

'Clive Brastow's plan solves no problem – only invents others.'

'Selling and giving the money to the World Council of Churches . . .'

'Is mad. In the circumstances quite mad. In any case, I consider that particular organisation as politically . . . curious.'

'I think your stance is very proper, Chancellor. Let me ask you.' Nutkin hesitated long enough to impress import. 'What kind of sum would you entertain from a British buyer?'

'Half a million. With proper safeguards. So he couldn't sell to America next day. Or ever.'

Nutkin frowned. The answer had been prompt and evidently well considered: the amount he thought too low – and too obtainable. Before he could comment Olive Merit entered the room.

The Chancellor's spinster sister was twelve years his junior. She kept house for him, and taught part-time at one of the town schools. She was a plain, athletic, lively woman of medium height and – in contrast to her brother – thin, sharp-featured, and little concerned about her personal appearance. Her hair was cut short like a man's. She was wearing a wool dress in what could best be described as serviceable grey.

'Evening, Miles. Thought I heard your dulcet tones,' she opened heartily. 'You going to want supper?'

'Thank you, no. I must go quite soon. Diana's expecting me home shortly.'

'That's good. About supper, I mean. Don't have much in the house. Never do Thursdays. You'd have been welcome, of course. More sherry?'

'You're a little early this evening, Olive.' This was Merit. 'We were discussing Chapter business,' he added pointedly.

'Well, don't mind me. Any news?' She picked up the evening newspaper and glanced down the front page, then looked up sharply. 'Oh, would you rather I left you to it?'

The Chancellor gave Nutkin a half-smile. 'I think we've covered the point.' His sister could be very obtuse at times. Later he would remind himself she was also an excellent cook, better than most professionals, and a great deal cheaper. 'You'll do what you can tomorrow, Miles? With the visitor? Before the meeting?'

'To try to bring him back to our way of thinking? Certainly.'

'Had you thought of calling on him first thing?'

'I hadn't. D'you want me to, Chancellor?'

'Not at all,' Merit came back quickly, adding, 'Whatever you think appropriate . . . Mr Chapter Clerk.'

'You two are very formal this evening. I suppose the Dean didn't win anyone round – at the meeting?' Olive Merit, sitting on the side of the desk, lifted her head from the paper and looked from one to the other. Neither man responded. 'Thought not. So it all hangs on Mark Treasure? Knew that name was familiar. Realised why today. I was at school with his wife. We were great chums. Is she coming, too?'

'I think not,' answered Nutkin.

'Well, if you were talking about him, Algy, perhaps you'd better send me to have breakfast with him, not Miles. He likes attractive birds.' She made a kind of snoring noise – the usual notice that a laugh was emerging.

Nutkin looked uncomfortable, sucked in air, and prepared to leave. The Chancellor looked thoughtful.

It was fifteen minutes later, at a quarter to seven, when Laura Purse admitted the well-built Minor Canon Twist into her flat and her welcoming arms. Although a cathedral official, she didn't qualify for a privileged apartment in Abbot's Cloister: Gerard Twist did – but he dined out as often as invited.

The flat was a conversion above the bookshop in North Street – one large living room, bedroom, small kitchen and even smaller bathroom. It was warm, well decorated and cosily furnished – even expensively so, taking the tenant's salary into account.

Laura was twenty-seven, a graduate and a qualified librarian-archivist. She was blonde, tallish, and strikingly attractive with more than a hint of Scandinavian lineage. She was even more intelligent than people guessed – and quite determined to marry Gerard Twist in his own best interests.

He kissed her affectionately – on the cheek: Gerard never risked throat infections, and in any case he was shy with women. He enjoyed the way Laura responded. She never made him feel uncomfortable. He wanted their relationship to go on deepening and was happy to have her make the pace.

Early on she had made it very plain she didn't hold with sex outside marriage, not in any circumstances. This had pleased Gerard: Laura had thought it would.

'Your hands are cold,' he said as she took his coat at the bottom of the stairs. 'You only just got back?'

'No. Been here ages. I'm cleaning potatoes. Hope you're hungry. Is there any more news?'

'Same as I told you. Decision at the meeting in the morning. I don't believe they'll sell. Not unless this banker changes his mind.'

'And there's no reason why he should?' When they reached the living room she went back to the kitchen.

He moved across to the stack of records beside her record-player.

'Told you, I've no idea. Maybe the Dean will get at him.' He looked strained. 'Where's the Fourth Brandenburg?'

'There somewhere. Do we have to have the Fourth again?'

'No. Which would you like?'

'Put the Third on, then,' she called. It was what had first endeared him to her: he did whatever she wanted – that and his heavenly voice, and his good looks, and his harmless conceits and remarkable contentment. Three years earlier, before she came to Litchester, she'd ended a torrid affair with a thrusting, ambitious man about as different from this one as it was possible to be – a man who had chosen her. She had gone to enormous pains choosing Gerard for herself.

'It'll mean the choir school folding, probably. That'll be half my job gone. There won't be the money for the organ. Donald Welt's pretty depressed.' He put the record on the player. 'D'you think they'll keep me on?'

'Being here is what you want, isn't it?' She had appeared around the kitchen door. 'Singing the services? Running the choir? Teaching the school? *Really* what you want?'

'I feel it's my vocation, yes. I don't believe I'd fit nearly so well running a parish, for instance. Yes, what I want is here. Not very ambitious. D'you think I'm right?'

'I'm sure you are. Don't worry, darling. I still believe things will come right.' And she meant it – above all, to keep her future husband and the father of her children contented.

# Chapter Four

'Could mean my resignation.' The bearded jaw dropped after he had spoken, but the face he made was one of only mild concern.

'Your what, dear?' Ursula Brastow had heard her husband well enough: simply she wasn't ready with an answer. He couldn't mean her to treat the matter lightly . . . not after . . . not possibly.

Canon Brastow cleared his throat – or tried to, 'Sorry, it's quite painful. Resignation,' he repeated. 'If we should agree to sell the Magna Carta.' He swallowed more of the hot soup. 'The principle involved would be too big to shirk. And if my view wasn't accepted. I've been thinking, it'd make it difficult to carry on as Treasurer.'

'I understand.' He couldn't compromise? She bit her lip on the thought and didn't utter the question.

Ursula was a small, round, and normally balanced woman – but recently she had been in the grip of an acute depression: the pills had been meant to cure her, except now her doctor wanted her to see an analyst. She hadn't told Clive.

She had met her husband in West Africa – in the mission field. She had been a nurse. It had been a sound match. People had said they made a fine team. And when they'd come back to England the future had looked every bit as fulfilling.

Her background had been quite different from his – not nearly such a good educational grounding. She hadn't had much to fall back on now the boys had gone.

There were two sons. One had just been ordained, the other was a medical student. She missed them. She was four years older than Clive – which had never mattered, until this year. Now it was one of the silly little things that seemed to be building barriers between them in her mind. She was just fifty-three.

'It'd be over a million pounds, you see? That's more than it's insured for even now. I told you about that, didn't I?' He watched her nodded reply then went on. 'Conscience surely demands the money would have to go where there's no other source of help. It's too easy for us – getting it this way. In fairness, that's why Ewart Jones has been against selling at all. So far.'

'But the vote is still expected to be against selling,' she offered limply. Why did she feel so inadequate – even now after what she'd done? 'More soup, dear?' She had made the soup herself: that was somehow a comfort.

It was a few minutes before seven. They always had supper early, and in the kitchen. Their meals were usually frugal and, unlike this evening, often shared with less fortunate people.

'Thanks. It's good. Is it cauliflower cheese I smell next? Don't know how you do these things in the time.' She had come in after him. She had told him she'd been out but he'd been preoccupied at the time and forgotten where.

'Made it before I went out.' She showed eager pleasure at the compliment.

The house, though not immense, they considered too big for the two of them. They had roughly arranged it so that the big basement was available as a temporary flat for the homeless or for refugees. It was empty at the moment, and people never seemed to stay in it for long, no matter how desperate they were when they arrived. The Brastows reasoned that the space wasn't ideal for the purpose – nor did they have the authority and the money to make it so with structural alterations. At worst they felt what they had arranged set an example. Their dining room was lent to a famine relief charity as a regional office.

'The Dean's working hard on Ewart Jones. He may still come round to selling. And I can't possibly vote against. All that money for a useless artefact.' He shrugged. 'It'd be mad to turn it down.'

'The cathedral needs money, of course.' After she'd said it she wished she hadn't. He was Treasurer: he knew the facts better than anyone. His unguarded facial reaction she interpreted properly as irritation at her stupidity: he corrected it quickly but too late.

'The Finance Committee's plan for a Cathedral Appeal still stands.' He poured himself some water. 'Ewart Jones supports it. We'd be aiming for three million. I think we'd get it, too. The Dean's doubtful. Ewart believes we ought to use professional fund-raisers for that. Wouldn't be surprised if Algy Merit thinks the same.'

'Don't professionals charge a lot?'

'About ten per cent of what they raise. There'd be a fee at the start. Non returnable. Ewart says it's only ten per cent of money we wouldn't otherwise have. It's one way of looking at it.'

'But you don't approve?'

'No.' He frowned. 'Not for a totally logical reason. Makes me feel uncomfortable. Like this wretched throat. In any case, all that's for future debate. The Magna Carta decision's on us tomorrow.'

'And Mr Treasure from London? You said . . .'

'Is against selling. So far as we know. He could change his mind.'

She hoped not: not after what she'd done. There were times in the day when the pills she took gave her courage enough for anything: now wasn't one of those times. A dreadful apprehension was clawing through her.


At ten past seven Canon Jones left his house for the second time since he had come in after evensong. He was wearing an overcoat – and concealed beneath it, across his chest, he was holding an oversized soft-leather document-case.

'Shan't be long, Nancy,' he'd called to his wife, who was busy in the kitchen. 'Note to deliver in the close.'

'Thought you'd done that,' she answered.

'This is another one.'

'All right. Dinner is half an hour. Glynis should be home by then.'

The note in his hand was for the Dean and could easily have

waited until morning. He dropped it into the Deanery letter box as he passed, then hurried onwards. He adjusted the set of the case under his coat while humming the tune of 'Ding, Dong, Merrily on High' which had been in his mind since he heard the choir practising it with the other Christmas music that morning.

The close seemed conveniently deserted. Most of the populace of this very provincial English town would be indoors having supper or watching television.

As he approached the east end of the cathedral he debated whether it was worth the diversion to use the cloister door when his destination was the Old Library over the north porch. But when it came to it discretion won, and he turned left, then right again, to follow the path that rounded the side of the Lady Chapel and then led to the south transept. It wouldn't do to chance being seen as he went in.

He had no misgivings about his plan. No doubt it was impetuous – but he'd always been that. Just as certainly it would wake people up to their obligations. So it was risky. St Paul had taken diverse risks in good causes: the saint had also been a small man.

He turned right on entering the lamplit, covered cloister. The door which led into the south transept of the cathedral was before him in shadow. It marked the end of the eastern arcade of Abbot's Cloister quadrangle. He glanced back briefly. There was no one in sight as he went for the heavy key in his coat pocket. From habit, at the same time, he tried the door – lifting the ancient ironwork latch and pushing, in the fairly certain knowledge the door was locked. But it opened.

The Canon shook his head. Mr Pounder was supposed to lock the door behind him at six-fifteen. It wasn't the first time there'd been evidence the old fellow was getting beyond it. Of course, someone else with a key could have come in since the Dean's verger had gone home. In that case, though, the door should still have been locked from one side or the other – depending on whether the other person was still in the building or not.

It didn't suit Ewart Jones's purpose for someone else to be in the cathedral. He stepped inside and listened in the darkness. The silence seemed complete. He locked the door behind him quietly, preparing to go forward in the nearly pitch darkness with less immediate confidence than he had watched the blind Dean exercise hundreds of times over the same route.

The windows in aisle, triforium and clerestory provided little illumination at first. He had not intended using lights for fear of attracting attention from outside: this would also now help to establish if he really was alone.

He moved in a straight northerly course from the door towards the crossing beneath the great central tower, as his sight began to acclimatise. He looked to the right as he passed the top of the south choir aisle. The clergy, choir and vergers' vestries were there, but there were no lights coming from any of them. The organ loft on the far side of the choir was also in darkness. And these were all the parts of the building most likely to be visited after normal hours by people with keys. It seemed he was alone – and that Mr Pounder had been careless about locking up.

After the crossing, he moved down the centre of the stone-flagged nave between the rows of chairs he could still only scarcely distinguish, and marking his way by the great rose window in the west front. He turned right opposite the north door.

There were two spiral staircases leading to the Old Library above the great porch: they were enclosed in stone turrets on either side of the porch doors inside the cathedral. There was no access from outside. The upstairs area housed what was left of the old chained library as well as the Litchester Magna Carta. Visitors ascended by the right-hand staircase and came down by the left after walking past the exhibits – and always under the eye of a volunteer official cathedral guide or one of the vergers. On Mondays to Thursdays after evensong Mr Pounder did the supervising there from five-thirty to six. Later he locked the turret doors at the top of the stairways and, after ensuring the building was empty, locked the cathedral itself, leaving through the cloisters.

Canon Jones reached for the key as he still half-felt his way to the turret on the left, then began mounting the steep stairs. It wasn't surprising Pounder was failing in the job, he ruminated. The fellow was too old for these stairs to begin with.

It was as he was trying to find the keyhole in the blackness that he sensed danger: smelt it. The door opened backwards on to the wide landing step, but he'd forgotten that. He had started by pushing inwards on it but it hadn't yielded. Then he tried to hurry with the unlocking except the key seemed not to affect anything.

'Mr Pounder, are you in there?' he cried at the top of his voice while wrestling with the key and a dreadful premonition. He knew the question was stupid. Why should Pounder still be there – behind a locked door? 'Don't worry, I'm coming,' he persisted. And now he really was alarmed, capable of mouthing any comforting inanity. 'I'm coming, Mr Pounder.'

It was as he shouted the last reassurance that his hand fell on the latch and he realised his error. He lifted the latch. Immediately the door flew back and propelled Canon Jones down the stairs like a bullet from a gun.

It was two hours later when Mark Treasure alighted from the train at Litchester's imposing, red-brick and distinctly Victorian railway station. There was only one other passenger getting off – a small man in a hurry and a bowler hat. There was no one getting on.

The banker had travelled all the way in the dining car. There he had been the sole customer, waited on by an over-attentive staff maniacally anxious to please and to preserve a still surviving member of an evidently dying breed.

There were a few – a very few – other people still on the train, he noticed, as he strode past four carriages on his way to the platform exit. Some would be Shrewsbury and others for Chester. It seemed British Rail was about to reroute this train – via busy Wolverhampton instead of sleepy Litchester. The chief steward had been predicting the event through four courses. The new service was expected to have a refreshment bar and not a dining car. 'There's not the quality of traveller any more, sir,' had been the pointed complaint, while narrowed eyes had been fixed on Treasure's calculating of the tip. The chief steward had repeated the lament later, and more wistfully, as part of a deeply respectful fare-well address incorporating heartfelt best wishes for Christmas.

'You're Mr Mark Treasure?' asked the girl. The question came more with the assurance of an already verified statement. Not to have been Mr Mark Treasure, he felt, would have been a serious shortcoming on his part. The man in the bowler hat had gone through the ticket barrier ahead of him without being quizzed.

'Afraid so,' he answered genially while considering his dark, petite interrogator. She was standing on the platform just in front of the ticket collector and his booth. He guessed she was in her early twenties. She was pert, alert, very pretty, with Cupid's-bow lips, a turned-up nose and an antipodean accent. She was wearing a thick-knit sweater with a deep halter collar, a tweed skirt, wool stockings and brogues – in shades of brown – and a long white scarf draped not turned about her neck. The small white terrier dog on the end of the lead in her left hand was already sniffing at Treasure's shoes.

'I'm Glynis Jones. Glad to know you, Mr Treasure.' The right hand stopped pulling on the scarf and got presented for shaking on the end of a very straight arm. 'My dog's called Jingles. She's a Jack Russell and very friendly.' The animal looked up at the mention of her name, head on one side, then went back to licking a toecap as earnest of the advertised good nature.

Treasure's forehead wrinkled. 'So you'll be . . . Canon Jones's daughter?' After shaking hands he bent down to pat Jingles. The animal snapped at him then, reputation in tatters, retreated behind Miss Jones, the bell on the dog collar emitting a worried accom-paniment.

'Bit nervous with strangers. She'll get used to you. Smart of you to figure who I was.' The girl dipped her chin self-consciously.

'It was my turn. And not too difficult.' Miss Gaunt, his secre-tary, had provided short biographies and family details on all members of the Chapter. 'Good of you to meet me.' He presented his ticket for clipping.

'Mummy and I thought someone should. Everybody else is pretty occupied. There's been an accident. And a fire. Earlier this evening. At the cathedral.' She had led him through the barrier and out on the huge, brick-paved station yard. 'Station's on the edge of town. There's never more than one taxi meets this train. You might have missed it.'

'I seem to have done just that.' They both watched the other passenger get into a Ford on the otherwise empty cab-rank. 'About the accident and the fire – anyone hurt?'

'My dad. He's OK,' she added quickly. 'Mr Pounder, the Dean's verger, I'm afraid he's dead. In the fire. It was pretty disastrous. In every way. Your journey's probably been a waste of time, too. Like to get in?' She unlocked the nearside door of a green, soft-top Suzuki four-wheel drive with a somewhat military appearance. Jingles, released, leapt smartly on to the front passenger-seat. There was a momentary pitting of wills before Treasure, who liked dogs, succeeded in banishing this one to the rear seat along with his bag. He examined the car's interior with a look of tolerant interest.

The girl noted the appraisal. 'I'm a farm secretary. This buggy gets me anywhere. Care to have the roof down?'

'Thank you, no. Not unless we're called to battle stations. Please go on about the cathedral.'

She strapped herself into the driving seat and started the motor. 'The Old Library caught fire. Dad discovered it. Got blown down some steps in the process. Thinks he was knocked out. For a moment. Still raised the alarm. They stopped the fire spreading. Old Library's pretty burnt. Except they saved the roof. Timbers badly charred.' Matching her staccato phrases, she moved the car off with a lurch.'

'The Old Library? That's above the porch, isn't it? Where the Magna Carta's kept? Was it damaged?'

'Burnt to a cinder. And the chained library books. Mr Pounder was in there. He was a very old man.' At the end of the yard she turned the car to the right into a wide thoroughfare. It was only sparsely built-up but the lights of the town centre showed a quarter of a mile ahead.

'Do they know how it started?'

'Pretty certainly. Mr Pounder was using a paraffin-stove heater. Old-fashioned kind. He shouldn't have had it. He felt the cold a lot.'

'And it tipped over?'

'That's the likeliest explanation.'

'Wonder why he didn't get out? Raise the alarm?'

'Could have tripped and fallen. Maybe fell over the stove. He was laid out on the floor when they found him. Pretty charred.'

He heard her swallow after the last phrase. He was also conscious of Jingles's nose pushing a way from the rear under the arm of his sheepskin coat. 'And your father?'

'Was in the cathedral. He smelled fire. Opened the door. The flames and smoke rushed out.'

'And blew him over?'

'That's about it. He got back, though, and shut the door. They're saying already he saved the cathedral.'

'By containing the fire, of course. Good thinking. And Mr Pounder . . .'

'Is the problem. Dad wasn't sure he was in there. Couldn't get in to look in any case. Except now he wishes he could have. Somehow.'

'Was Mr Pounder usually there at – what time was it?'

'Bit after seven-fifteen. No. He used to open the Old Library for half an hour at five-thirty. For any visitors after evensong. Usually there aren't any. Not this time of year. But he'd been doing it like for ever. Matter of pride, I suppose.'

'Despite the cold.' Now the little Jack Russell's head had emerged through the crook of Treasure's arm.

'That's right. Anyhow, his job was to lock the library at six, check everything else in the cathedral was locked, then go round with a handbell.'

'A handbell?'

'Wakes up anyone asleep in a dark corner at closing time.'

'I see.'

'He was supposed to leave the building by six-fifteen. The police take responsibility for security then.'

'So your father could reasonably suppose Mr Pounder had left?'

'Except the door Dad used to get in wasn't locked. Mr Pounder should have locked it behind him. Dad thought he'd forgotten. He'd been forgetting plenty of things lately.'

Treasure nodded. 'And you're sure the Magna Carta's lost?'

'Along with everything else, like the chained books. I think everything was insured.'

'Was it a big chained library?'

'Quite small. Only one combined bookcase and reading desk. Restored fourteenth-century original. And a few big manuscript books attached to it by chains. About a dozen. Not valuable. It was just to show what a medieval chained library looked like.'

'The Litchester chained library used to be quite big, I thought?'

'Never as big as Hereford. The one here was broken up. Most of the best books, the ones used for research, they've been rebound. They're in the New Library. In the cloisters.'

'That's a blessing. I wonder if . . .'

'Sorry. You are staying at the Red Dragon?' the girl interrupted. They had passed through a tangle of narrow one-way streets lined with shops ablaze with light and Christmas displays. Now they had emerged at the top end of the wider but also one-way Bridge Street.

'Yes. It's on the right over there, isn't it? Years since I was here. Still a lot of activity, I see.'

There were a great many vehicles parked along the street, including a BBC Television outside-broadcast van. A crowd of several hundred people was gathered behind police-controlled barriers at the entrance to the cathedral close lower down and on the other side of the street from the hotel. Beyond, the west end of the great edifice was illuminated inside and out. The outline of the nave and central tower were also clearly definable against the sky and over the top of the low street buildings.

'You should have seen it an hour ago,' Miss Jones commented as they drew up outside the long, Georgian and rendered façade of the Red Dragon.

'D'you suppose I'll be allowed in the close?'

'You will if you're with me. I live there. Want me to wait while you check in? You'd better do that now. They're going to be full tonight.'

'Thanks.' He paused before getting out, studying the cathedral. Jingles, now sitting on his lap, gave the appearance of doing the same but looked back at him alertly from time to time. 'Tragic about your Mr Pounder, but I'd think what you were saying is right. Your father probably saved the building. The priceless building. Why was he in there?'

She switched off the engine. 'When they asked him, he couldn't remember.'

'Act of God, maybe?'

She didn't reply.

# Chapter Five

Chief Officer Olley, in charge of the now departed fire tenders, blew his nose sharply. Like the rest of Olley, the nose was remarkably large and robust, making a seemingly appropriate appendage for one whose professional activities involved the detecting of volatile emissions.

'Isolated bit of the building, you see? Would have been a lot worse in any other part,' he said, looking from Treasure to Miles Nutkin and then to Percy Bliter, who nodded knowingly. The four were standing in the cathedral close in front of the north porch. Several other knots of concerned people were close by, as well as numbers of bored policemen.

There was plenty of light from regular and auxiliary sources to show the extent of the outside damage.

The square porch jutted out some twenty feet from the north aisle of the nave. At ground level on three sides it presented squat, semi-circular entrance arches decorated with dogtooth carvings above scalloped capitals. At the second level those openings were matched by pairs of round-headed windows. Heavy stepped buttresses supported the extension at the two leading corners. The roof was out of sight behind a straight cornice.

The lower storey looked untouched by the fire, but above there was a great deal of scorching to the stone-work. Some of the windows had had their lattices of tiny diamond-shaped panes shattered. Where the glass in them remained it was cracked and blackened.

'It's a wooden roof?' This was Treasure. Fifteen minutes earlier he had been introduced to Nutkin by Glynis Jones, who had left them together. Since then – shepherded by the Chapter Clerk – he had been inside the cathedral and met the people he was with now. He had also been introduced to the Dean and his wife, to Canon Brastow, Mr Smithson-Bows the diocesan architect, and numbers of other cathedral dignitaries. Some had clearly been lingering at the scene more because they would have felt guilty at quitting it than because there was anything for them still to see or do that night.

'Roof is wood under lead, yes,' said the fireman. 'Another few minutes it would have gone up properly. Good thing the floor's flagstone.'

'But there was a good deal of wood in the room?'

'Yes, Mr Treasure.' It was Bliter who answered. 'Most of the fittings.' He glanced at Nutkin as though seeking permission to continue. 'We'd never have allowed paraffin near the area. Not if we'd known.'

'And the smoke-detector system? I gather . . .'

'Covers the whole building except the crypt and the Old Library, I'm afraid,' Nutkin put in. 'At the time it was installed those responsible had to make some savings.' He shook his head to indicate he hadn't been one of the cost-cutting band.

'False economy, of course,' said Olley.

'Your predecessor had to approve it.' Bliter sounded sure of his ground.

'Sometimes we have to countenance things like that,' answered the officer, putting the emphasis on the longest word. 'Likely there was no alternative. If there wasn't enough money. Half a warning system being better than none at all.'

'I wonder if the insurers took the same view,' injected Treasure, who happened to be chairman of a very large insurance company.

'They're entirely satisfied with our security arrangements,' affirmed the Cathedral Administrator. 'They know human observers usually beat mechanical ones every time.'

The confidence in this comment was somewhat undermined by the questioning glance Chief Officer Olley directed at the charred

Old Library, and before he observed: 'They'll have an inspector here in the morning, no doubt.'

'Meantime the structure's safe?'

'Yes, Mr Treasure,' the fireman confirmed. 'No need for shoring up or anything like that, Mr Smithson-Bows said.'

'He's arranging for the roof timbers to be properly examined in the morning. It's likely there'll have to be scaffolding when they're made good.' This was Bliter in an ebullient tone of voice meant to impress that he was looking ahead with confidence.

Treasure shook his head. 'Curious no one spotted the fire from the outside earlier.'

'Very few people about after six,' said Nutkin promptly.

'Paraffin can burn very dirty,' Olley observed. 'Could have blacked up those windows pretty fast.'

'And you think Mr Pounder knocked over the heater?'

'The Magna Carta display case as well possibly,' the fireman replied. 'It's a small area. All those wooden fitments, and a bit of carpet where it could do the most harm. Acted like a wick. Be up to the official enquiry to decide, of course, but that's what likely happened. Pounder was lying right by the heater – and the Dean's mace.'

'Why would he have taken the mace up there?'

'He shouldn't, Mr Treasure.' This was Nutkin. 'He was supposed only to carry it in procession in front of the Dean.'

'He liked to show it off. As an extra exhibit when he was in charge of the Old Library,' offered Bliter.

'Another of his private arrangements,' said the Chapter Clerk stiffly.

'Like the paraffin heater.' Olley frowned as he spoke. 'Beats me no one knew about that. Probably kept it in the cupboard up there. Wooden cupboard. What's left of it. Where we found the empty paraffin-can. Unbelievable.'

'People did know about it.' The firm statement came from immediately behind the group, which was arranged in a semicircle. The tone was guttural, the accent local and uncultured. The speaker was a dark thickset man, middle-aged and middle height. He was wearing a short topcoat with leather patchings.

'Good evening, Jakes,' said Bliter brusquely in the tone of a noble grudgingly acknowledging a serf. 'Very sorry about your father-in-law,' he conceded further, but made no attempt at introductions.

'You the Mr Jakes married to Mr Pounder's daughter?' enquired Olley.

'Right.'

'Mr Jakes is head cathedral gardener,' Nutkin vouchsafed to Treasure.

'You say people knew about the paraffin stove, Mr Jakes?' This was Olley again.

'Of course they did. Stands to reason. Couldn't go through without seeing it.'

'Visitors,' said Bliter in a final sort of way.

'And others. Staff.'

'Not to my knowledge. It was never reported to me.' The Administrator was now more addressing the Chapter Clerk than the head gardener.

'Felt the cold something terrible, he did. More this year. Wouldn't take in an electric fire, though. Wouldn't use the cathedral power. He was that honest. I told him he shouldn't be using paraffin.'

'I'm glad to hear it, Mr Jakes,' said Nutkin.

'My wife's that cut up. He lived with us. The old man.' For some reason Jakes was putting his points to Treasure. 'The wife says he most probably had a heart attack. Fell on the stove.'

'That's possible,' said Olley and blew his nose again.

'Know soon enough. When they've done the post-mortem. But it's not right he gets all the blame, though. That's what the wife says, and I agree with her. He had permission for that stove.'

'Who from?' asked the fireman.

'Not for me to say,' Jakes answered, looked hard at Treasure, hesitated, then swung about and stumped off.

The Honourable Mrs Margaret Elizabeth Hitt, the Dean's wife, was approaching sixty with dignity and serenity. The daughter of a viscount – hence the courtesy title – she had the features and bearing of a true aristocrat with the height to augment both. In her day she had been a beauty – and might have been a celebrated debutante had she been at all attracted to charades. Instead she had graduated in English and married a blind clergyman after concluding she needed him more than he needed her. Subsequently she had applied boundless energies to being an exceptional wife, mother and universal aunt, as well as a formidable church-woman, a noted writer of historical fiction and a still useful tennis-player.

'More coffee, Mr Treasure?' she encouraged, 'it's decaffein- ated.'

'Thank you, it's very good coffee.' Treasure leant across with his cup from a chintzy armchair beside the fireplace. The Dean was opposite him, and Mrs Hitt was on the sofa facing the log fire.

The high-ceilinged, long and well-proportioned drawing room was furnished with a great deal of style but also with an eye to the practicalities. There were some fine antique pieces and a number of good pictures. A Bechstein grand piano dominated one end of the room. Treasure accepted that the absence of occasional rugs and the relative absence of bric-à-brac, small tables, fragile lamps and other lightweight impedimenta was a mild concession to the Dean's blindness – but only after Hitt himself had called attention to the fact. 'No bull-traps in this room,' he had remarked as they entered ten minutes earlier: there was no hesitation, either, in the way the cleric moved about here.

'Your room all right at the hotel?'

'Seems fine, Dean. I only stopped to undo my bag.'

'What number?'

'Eh . . . three-twenty.'

'One of the best,' the other man confirmed. 'Third floor at the back. Renovated last year. No outside noise. Away from an in- describably noisy lift, and next to the fire escape. Whole place is a charming death-trap, of course. But, then, you can't have every- thing.'

Mrs Hitt smiled. 'It's not that bad. We know it well because we put a lot of people up there. This house looks large but it isn't. Only one decent guest-room and an antiquated bathroom some way off. Even so, you'll have the option to stay next time, now you know the worst.'

'Thank you. With no Magna Carta I'm afraid I shall have even less reason for visiting Litchester than I had before.'

'Well, I'm very glad you decided to drop in now,' Hitt observed pointedly. He had invited Treasure to do so when they had met in the close. 'Good to know where you'd have stood over the Magna Carta sale.'

'It was a change of mind, Mr Treasure?'

'Yes, Mrs Hitt. Bit academic now, of course.' He took a sip of the brandy he had accepted with the first cup of coffee.

'Not entirely. Gives the sellers the moral ascendancy,' said the Dean.

'That's you and Canon Brastow.'

'The Treasurer and me, yes. Algy Merit and Ewart Jones —'

'The Chancellor and the Precentor?'

'That's right. They were against selling. Now, of course, it's simply a matter of what we do with the insurance money.'

'Rather less than £1.1 million the sale would have brought.'

'At a million? Not that much less.'

Treasure frowned. 'I understood from Nutkin it was insured for five hundred thousand.'

'It was till four weeks ago. After the American offer hardened we increased it to a million. When they put all that money on call, and made tomorrow the deadline.'

'Did Nutkin know about the insurance?'

'No reason why he shouldn't have.' The Dean paused to reflect. 'On the other hand, perhaps he didn't. It was something Clive Brastow and I decided on here one morning. Window-dressing in a way.'

'You mean if the bidder put a seven-figure valuation on the thing you felt you should, too?'

'Something of the kind, yes. I remember Clive rang Percy Miter

47

at the Chapter House. Told him to fix it with our broker. Small matter at the time. Small premium.'

'Small premium?'

'For the period involved, I imagine. We both of us assumed the sale would go through in a matter of weeks. Seemed inefficient not to have the cover right. In case of accidents. I think it was Clive's idea. One of his better ones.'

'He'll still make problems on what's to be done with the money. Has it earmarked for Third World relief.' This was Margaret Hitt. 'Curious. He simply won't recognise the cathedral needs relieving.' She smiled and then recited, '"Let no one try to say the flesh is more important than old stones. It's a false analogy. Administrative sophistry. Like saying St Paul's is less valuable than a cure for cancer."' She paused. 'Isn't that terribly true?'

'Yes. Who said it?' asked the banker. 'No, let me guess. John Betjeman, I expect.' He was pleased by her affirming nod.

'Wrote it, not said it. In a letter to a friend of ours. About the fate of Norwich churches. He wasn't knocking the need for cancer cures, of course. Only begging for a right perspective.'

'Certainly applies here,' offered the Dean with spirit. 'Clive Brastow's a very saintly person,' said Mrs Hitt. 'So is Ursula, his wife.'

Treasure made as if to say something but hesitated. Gilbert Hitt got in before him with: 'Estimable pair. Yes, saintly probably. Which makes them the very devil to live with sometimes.' He sniffed. 'Now I've shocked Treasure, I expect.'

'Not at all, Dean. Since there's been an accident, though . . .'

'I agree we should all be grateful for Clive's perspicacity. Been thinking that all evening.'

'Can you overrule him on how the money's used?'

'Won't be necessary. Algy Merit and Ewart Jones were simply against the sale of the Magna Carta. They'll have no inhibitions about the right way to use insurance money.'

'Neither should I, although I don't come into it any more.' This was Treasure. 'It seems the responsibilities of the vicar's warden at the church of Great St Agnes have been utterly discharged by the fire.' He swirled the brandy in his glass before adding, 'I suppose I could propose we buy another Magna Carta with the money.'

A look of horror appeared on the Dean's face. 'You won't, of course?'

'Mr Treasure's joking,' his wife put in.

'And if I weren't it wouldn't matter. There wouldn't be an early exemplification for sale at any price. They're pretty rare.'

'We might find a fake,' offered the other man unexpectedly. 'In theory we'd be in the right place. I remember Pounder saying years ago they produced them by the yard here. In the seventeenth century.' His expression saddened. 'Poor old Pounder. I'll miss him dreadfully.'

'Good innings, though,' said Margaret Hitt cheerfully. 'They say he was well over eighty. Let's hope it was a painless end.'

'He was against the sale. We never discussed it directly.' The Dean smiled and shook his head. 'He made the point with heavy inferences. Or, rather, what he imagined were oblique references to my cupidity in the matter.'

'Commander Bliter told me he'd have defended that Magna Carta with his life.'

The Dean considered Treasure's words for a moment before replying. 'Possibly true. Certainly he'll be writhing in paradise now for causing its destruction.'

'Was there a charge to view the Old Library?'

'No.' It was Mrs Hitt who replied. 'There should have been, but Mr Pounder, for one, would certainly have objected.'

'And since he and a few other elderly volunteers supervised through the opening times for nothing . . .' The Dean punctuated his remark with a shrug. 'Pounder used to cover that late session four days a week, you know?'

'Sitting in a draughty room with both doors open,' added his wife.

'Would they have been open?' This was Treasure.

'Not tonight. Not on Thursdays for some reason,' the Dean answered. 'They were closed when Ewart Jones and I left the cathedral. Pounder was *in situ* by then.'

'Did you go up the stairs?'

'No.'

'My husband has a disarming way of seeing or, rather, hearing round corners,' Margaret Hitt put in promptly. 'Or up spiral staircases, as in this case.'

'Anyone can do it who keeps his eyes closed and his ears open,' said the Dean dismissively. 'Blind people get the most practice. It's to do with vibrations.'

'Would he have kept the doors closed when he had that heater on? To stop anyone smelling the paraffin?' asked the banker.

The Dean shook his head. 'Not a hope of that. He did it to keep the warmth in, I expect.' He made a soft whistling noise through his teeth.

'Gilbert means a blind person also develops an acute sense of smell,' said Margaret Hitt with what the banker deemed to be surprising frankness. 'More brandy, Mr Treasure?' she asked.

'And what exactly does a farm secretary do?' asked Treasure as he and Glynis Jones walked westwards across the cathedral close. It was just after eleven. The two had run into each other as the banker had been leaving the Deanery. Canon Jones's daughter had come out to exercise Jingles, who was now trotting several paces ahead of them.

'Broadly, I'm in charge of accounts. Depreciation. VAT. The works. Currently for nineteen farmers. Various sizes but mostly small to medium. Each client gets about a day a month. Except it's not so neat in practice. I handle wages for all of them. Farmworkers like to be paid in cash. On Fridays. Fridays are hairy.'

'You're self-employed?'

'You bet. Each client pays me a fee. Quarterly. Most of it in advance.'

'Did you qualify in accountancy?'

'I'm in the process. Don't have to. I can cope without. I've done a farm secretary diploma course.'

'There is one?'

'Sure. Two years at an agricultural college. Better value than a degree in sociology, for instance. Useful if I marry a farmer too.'

'You planning to?'

'Not straight away. Eventually, maybe. Back home in New Zealand. Hello, why all the renewed action, I wonder?'

The two had nearly reached the north porch when a police van drew up there. It had been driven along the pedestrian pathway from Bridge Street. Six uniformed policemen got out of it. Under the direction of a sergeant, they began arranging a semi-circular cordon of steel barriers around the porch, and some yards out from it. Before this there had been only one lone policeman standing in the emptied close. Now a police car was coming along the path from the same direction as the van.

'What's going on, Sergeant?' Treasure enquired.

'Orders from the station, sir. This area to be closed off till further notice. Could I have your name, please.'

'Mr Treasure's with me, Peter.'

'Oh, hello, Glynis. Didn't recognise you. You'll have to move on, I'm afraid. It's residents only and no loitering for anyone in the close. Better put that dog on the lead. Excuse me.' The young sergeant stepped away to meet the two plainclothes men who had got out of the car. Jingles, inside forbidden territory, having sniffed the bases of the porch buttresses, liberally anointed the ground in front of the eastern one and scurried back to her mistress with head up and both ears cocked.

'The sergeant and I are both bellringers,' said Glynis, attaching a lead to the little terrier. 'What d'you think they're doing.'

'Evidently something they left undone before,' answered Treasure.

'I'd better tell Dad.' The girl looked and sounded disconcerted. 'Well, good night, Mr Treasure. See you tomorrow.' She turned about and hurried away.

The fresh activity at the cathedral wasn't reflected in deserted Bridge Street as Treasure made his way back to the Red Dragon. There were cars parked near the hotel, but the television van had gone. There were only a few people in the residents' lounge when he passed it on his way to the reception desk. The cathedral fire was not proving to be much of a crowd-keeper after all – not four hours after the event.

The night porter was in charge of the desk. 'Mr Mark Treasure is it, sir?' he asked when he was getting Treasure's key, and which the banker noted he could just as easily have reached for himself. 'Telephone message for you, sir.' He handed over an envelope which had already been opened. The room number typed on it had been altered in ink. 'Sorry, it was given to another guest by mistake, sir.'

Treasure read the word typed on the sheet of hotel message-paper. 'Doesn't say who it's from. D'you know if it was a man or a woman?'

'Couldn't say, sir. Telephonist might remember. Got a time on it, has it?'

'Yes. Nine-fifty.'

'Have to wait till tomorrow then, sir. The girls leave at ten. That'll be Daphne. The one who took that message. She'll be on again at four tomorrow afternoon. Funny she didn't get a name.'

'She might have thought she had. It's confusing.' And it's also meaningless, he added to himself as he read the message again in the lift. It said: 'Ask about the Magna Carta from Daras.'

# *Chapter Six*

'You reckon I can go home now, then?' asked Cindy Larks in a rich country burr. She was coming down the stairs still preening her shock of red hair. A big girl, Cindy was pretty in a rough-hewn, gypsy way. 'I'll stay if you like, of course.' She paused on the bottom step fixing Dr Donald Welt with what she imagined was a provocative smile. She dropped her hands on to her gently swaying hips. 'Why can't I ever stay all night?'

'Because you're not old enough.'

She advanced into the living room and put her arms around his neck. She was taller than the thirty-two-year-old bearded organist. He enjoyed the feel of her body – just as he admired her natural singing voice, but for less selfish or for more overtly commendable reasons.

'I'm plenty old enough. I'm eighteen. You know that.'

'Well, your mother wouldn't approve.'

'Go on. My mum couldn't care a . . .'

'It's better like this,' he interrupted. He couldn't say baldly that, despite her physical charms and compliant ways, he couldn't cope with any more of her inane conversation – especially not tonight. He was a man who compartmented his life – and his day: it was getting late, and he did his best composing around midnight. 'Just leave quietly. And try not to let anyone see you, there's a good girl.'

'If I was a good girl . . .' she began with a wicked grin.

'You are. And that's why you'll get to London. If you practise.' He began steering her towards the hall.

The house was part of the eastern terrace of Abbot's Cloister

53

– a row of monks' cells now converted as quarters for cathedral officials. It was small – two bed-rooms and a bathroom upstairs, a big living room and a well-equipped kitchen below.

'Can I come tomorrow as well? You said there'd be an extra lesson this week. To make up. And the other. You know? That's if you want.' She sniggered.

He nodded, thinking she was a sensible girl at heart: didn't make a nuisance of herself when she didn't get her own way. And he remembered he had promised an extra session because he'd be away next Thursday. 'Same as today, then,' he said. 'Seven-fifteen.'

'I could come straight after evensong. Give us more time like. You know?' She looked at him coyly – except coyness wasn't one of Cindy's convincing affectations.

'No,' he answered bluntly and knowing she wasn't going to argue over that, either. She knew which side her bread was buttered. He was doing a great deal to develop her voice and her singing career, which was more than could be said for Gerard Twist, who was shy of the girl choristers and put up with them only as an economic necessity.

Welt was sure the girl had a professional future as a mezzo-soprano – but not while she went on working at a check-out in a supermarket. He was giving her free singing lessons – and he had very nearly engineered her acceptance and a bursary at one of the London music colleges.

So, he rationalised again as he took down her coat, he earned his physical enjoyment of her. He had no conscience in the matter, and in precious few other matters. He had no conventional good intentions about an enduring relationship, and the girl knew it – this girl and several other girls.

He was given to explaining he would never remarry, that once had been enough, and that his single and consuming passion was the creation of music. His first musical play had been a critical success and a financial disaster – at the Edinburgh Festival: it had never reached London. The next would be more ambitious – and another two years in the writing and composing.

Meantime the income from his job at Litchester was important to him. So he didn't risk unnecessary gossip about his private life. He didn't let young women stay in his house all night, and he tried to avoid their leaving late. There were morality clauses in his contract and he suspected quite a few people around ready to invoke them, given the opportunity.

Tonight had invented special problems. He'd been called to the cathedral over the fire. Cindy had arrived before that. She'd shown curiously little interest in the event, and remained at the house. Although he had told her to slip away if he didn't return shortly, she'd been waiting for him when he got back – in his bedroom. He had found it hard to turn her out then, especially bearing in mind there had still been a good many people about.

'If I come earlier sometimes, I could make you a nice supper, you know?' she persisted as he helped her on with the coat. 'We get ever so many out-of-date frozen-food packs. At the shop. For nothing. For staff. TV meals. You know? They're all right. Only we can't sell them when they've expired. You know?'

And if she said 'you know' again he'd expire as well. 'Thanks, no,' he said aloud. 'I need to have supper alone. To think,' he added to avoid insult. She respected his intellect. 'I have it early. In the town.'

'Did you come back past the cathedral tonight?' she asked suddenly.

'Why?'

'Only you could have seen the fire.'

'Well, I didn't.' It was the first time she'd shown any concern with what had happened, except to say she was sorry about Pounder.

'If they get the money, the insurance, like you said, your job'll be OK, will it? Same as if they'd sold the Magna Carta?' She watched his frown deepen. 'Well, you said last week they might get a cheaper organist. Part-timer. If they packed up the choir school and didn't get the organ mended. You know? Wouldn't have been right, that. Not to my way of thinking. Wouldn't have been fair.'

He recalled telling her something of the kind. 'I'll be OK, yes. Anyway, you shouldn't worry about me.'

'I'm not. Not now, then.'

'Will you be putting the kettle on again, Mother? It's parched I am. Not surprising as well,' Patrick Duggan, the head verger, swayed uncertainly. He regularly addressed his wife as 'Mother'. He'd got into the habit of it years before when all the children were at home. Her name was Bridget, which he'd never cared about. For her own part she happily countenanced the constant reminder that she had been a fruitful wife – there had been five offspring – even if the memories of their begetting brought no joy to her at all.

Bridget, fifty-eight, but looking older, went out to the kitchen where they took their meals. Duggan stayed in the main room where she had been watching television with their youngest son Rory when her husband had come in. The house was on a council-owned estate on the far side of town from the cathedral.

Rory, a burly twenty-three, hadn't looked up when his father had entered. The young man was unemployable rather than unemployed – though he had been that, too, and fairly consistently since leaving school. He took jobs often enough and long enough to ensure he was entitled to national assistance in the far longer periods when he was idle. The dole constituted pocket money for Rory because fundamentally he lived off his parents – which saddened his mother, who could find no fault in her last-born, and infuriated his father, who couldn't stand the sight of him.

'Anybody else dead? Besides old Pounder?' Rory asked, then looked around suddenly. His eyes widened when he saw what his father was doing. 'Oh, yes? Come into money, have we? Christmas bonus already?'

Duggan stuffed the five-pound notes he'd been counting back into his pocket. 'None of your bloody business. It's earned money, so it is.' But he looked furtive all the same.

'Dirty Protestant money, is it? The wages of sin, to be sure.' The pronounced Southern Irish cadence didn't come naturally to

Rory as it did to Duggan. All the children had been born and brought up in Litchester. He thickened the accent and broadened the idiom to irritate his father. And the Protestant jibe came in the same context.

Except for Duggan himself, the family was Roman Catholic. Bridget actively practised the faith; Rory had not so much lapsed as never seriously joined.

Duggan had undergone self-conversion to the Church of England just before applying for a job in the cathedral forty years earlier. That was after he had served three years in the British Army. Already married at the time, he had crossed the Channel to volunteer near the end of the Second World War to enhance his prospects of peacetime employment in England later. The last expectation was only actually realised through the intervention of a service comrade, the much older Neville Pounder, who had already returned to his job at the cathedral. The friendship between the two had later foundered – like a number of similar attachments made during Duggan's time in the local Litchester Regiment, and due mostly to his penchant for borrowing money and failing to return it.

'If you must know, the money's me winnings,' he blurted out angrily, then wished he hadn't.

'Winnings, is it? With no racing all this week? Not anywhere on account of fog.' Rory turned about completely in the armchair he'd been straddling, the better to interrogate his father, who he sensed was fuddled with drink and hiding something.

'Dogs. Me winnings on the dogs. Ah, thanks, Mother.' Bridget had returned with a tray of tea things.

'Is it all settled now? At the cathedral. There's no more danger?' she asked.

'The fire's out. Hours ago now. They'll be looking to the damage in the morning.' He hiccupped loudly. 'It's a sad thing.'

'But we made some money on it.' This was Rory, who had been studying his father the whole time. 'Now, how did we do that?'

'Is that right, Patrick?' Bridget looked up from pouring his tea.

'No, it's not right. It's a . . . it's a foul invention. I collected me racing winnings tonight. And I nearly didn't.' His face screwed up as he concentrated. 'Because didn't I lose the ticket? Well, I found it again, except that'd made me late. Never had the time for checking the money.' He turned on his son. 'And didn't they fetch me straight from the pub when I got there? When the fire was on? And I've not been home since.'

'You were late in the pub, then?' said his wife quietly.

'They were big winnings,' Rory said, tiring of the baiting. He swung around again to watch what was on the screen – a repeat showing of a football match with the sound turned low.

Duggan sat on the sofa with his wife. He sipped the tea. He wasn't concentrating on the television, though.

'Got the offer of Neville Pounder's job,' he half-whispered, not intending Rory should hear, though he couldn't wait to announce the news to Bridget.

'Is that for sure, then?' she asked, and sounding unconvinced.

'Certain sure. The Commander himself. Just now.'

Duggan would be sixty-five – official retirement age – the following March. For years he had been angling to be first in line for Pounder's job when it became vacant. The Dean's verger was paid by honorarium – an annual fee, not a salary. It was part-time work and not pensionable, but it wasn't subject to an age limit, either.

'I can start straight away. Sure it'll be no problem doing the two jobs for a while.'

'And Mr Jakes isn't in for it at all?'

'Because it's not fitting work for a gardener. Wasn't I always saying that? Well, I was right.'

'But didn't Mr Pounder start as a gardener? You're certain the Dean himself will approve?' She still seemed doubtful and carefully watched her husband's reaction to the question. 'You were never his favourite man.'

'That's not true. Not any more. We're great friends. The Dean and me.' Duggan scowled at his tea; then, forgetting, he added in a louder voice, 'Anyway, the Commander's promised, so he has. He can't go back on a solemn promise.'

'And he threw in a fistful of fivers for good measure,' Rory piped up raucously after catching every word. 'So what does Commander Bliter owe you all of a sudden? Offering Pounder's job before the guy's cold. Is it bribery and corruption that's involved? Are you covering up something for the man?'

'You're not, are you, Patrick?' asked Bridget with a convincing show of no confidence.

'Towel, Percy. Pass me my towel,' commanded Jennifer Bliter from the bath. 'Why we always find ourselves together in this stupid little bathroom I'll never know.'

Bliter provided the towel and pulled up his sagging pyjama trousers. He continued cleaning his teeth, which absolved him from giving the obvious or any answer to her question.

Jennifer spent a good deal of time in the bathroom. Most particularly she spent the last half-hour of her waking day in the bath itself, nursing the gin and tonic which, with the warmth of the water, she was utterly convinced enabled her to sleep without the help of pills. And she was very probably right since the drink was invariably a very stiff one.

So unless he got to his own nightly ablutions ahead of his wife Bliter was obliged to join her in the bathroom or wait for up to thirty minutes. Tonight she had taken to the water just before he came home at eleven-thirty.

It was quite a small bathroom – like the house, which was nearly a replica of the one next door occupied by Dr Welt.

'Margaret Hitt has three bathrooms in the Deanery.' Jennifer wiped the moisture from her face, then settled in the water again.

'Plumbing there's pretty Balkan, though. Rather be here. These fittings are barely ten years old.' He answered almost automatically. He was used to heading off her comparisons with other people's allegedly superior living conditions, especially Mrs Hitt's. Jennifer considered herself to be on the same social and intellectual level as the Dean's wife – a palpably inaccurate conception, at least in the second context, but one which she had persisted with ever since the Bliters had come to Litchester.

'I watched the TV news. On three channels. You weren't on.' The statement came as an admonition. She adjusted her shower cap and picked up her glass from the chromium bathrack.

'There was only BBC. They had a broadcast unit in the area. The woman said they'd probably run my interview at breakfast time.' He wiped the condensation off the washbasin mirror so that he could see to brush his hair, some of which he was training to grow in a new direction.

'Miles Nutkin was on. With the architect.'

'That was earlier. I was busy.' Curious: she'd quickly lost interest in the damage, the death, the trouble he might have been in.

Jennifer pulled out the plug and stood up in the bath. With her husband present there was hardly room to stand anywhere else.

He snatched a glance at her in the mirror. She had worn well, though she had always been thin rather than slim. Physically she was still passable, at the right angle. Not that they much went in for a physical relationship any more. He brushed his hair a bit harder, while considering the depth of the physical relationship he might have been enjoying with Cindy Larks.

He had literally bumped into Cindy as he had turned into the cloister minutes earlier. It was always embarrassing for him to meet her alone – ever since the time at that crowded party. He had made a mild pass at her then, and got a frighteningly positive response. The temptation to follow up this success had been strong – nearly irresistible. He had resisted all the same. Was it his marriage that stopped him, or her age, or the fact he had guessed what was going on between Cindy and that swine Welt? In fact it was none of those things. Bliter actually preferred fantasy to reality: he wallowed in fantasy.

There was no possible doubt Cindy found him attractive. She made it obvious – every time he saw her, even fleetingly like tonight. He savoured again the questioning look. There had been no censure in it, only warmth – and a special promise in her eyes.

'It'll all come out, of course.'

He started guiltily from his reverie. 'I'm sorry?'

'I sometimes think you've gone deaf.' She pulled off the shower cap and fluffed up her shortish black hair, then stepped out of the bath. 'The paraffin heater. Aren't they bound to believe it caused the fire?' She opened the door and crossed the landing to their bedroom.

He followed, fantasy firmly dismissed. 'They believe it already. Suppose it'll have to be reported formally.'

'And the old fool had it there against regulations?' The admiral's daughter was strong on regulations. She dropped a white nylon nightdress over her head. 'And nobody knew it was there?'

'People might have done,' he offered carefully. 'But not consciously.'

'Didn't it smell?'

'Not from below in the nave.'

'What about anyone else going into the Old Library when it was on? They'd have known.'

'Nobody did go in. Probably not since the time he'd started feeling the cold. Would have been about a week, I'd think.'

'Not anybody? You mean he opened up the place for nothing?'

'In the winter, yes. There aren't any visitors after evensong. He did it for self-gratification. Made him feel needed.'

Jennifer got into one of the twin beds. 'You could still get away with it, then?'

'What d'you mean?' He stopped in the middle of putting on his pyjama jacket.

'Well, it's obviously your responsibility to see cathedral employees don't do stupid things. Difficult to stop what they do in secret, I suppose.'

'Not my direct responsibility, either. In a line way. Not my responsibility at all.'

'There's a chain of command over that kind of thing?'

'Certainly. If a verger's doing something wrong it's up to Duggan, the chief verger, to stop him.'

'That drunk? No one respects him.'

'He knew nothing about the heater.' Bliter ignored the last comment. 'He'll swear to it. So will the other three vergers,' he added with conviction.

# Chapter Seven

Treasure liked to breakfast well in a hotel. And he preferred going down for it in the restaurant. That way the coffee and toast were usually hotter and there was a bigger choice of everything.

At the Red Dragon the meal was a help-yourself affair. Silver serving dishes of hot foods were displayed on a buffet table. There was even a dish of the banker's favourite kedgeree. It was just after seven-thirty and there was only one other guest present – a short man sitting by himself in a corner.

'What's happened to all the reporters and camera men?' Treasure had asked of the large, motherly woman in the black dress in charge of the buffet.

'Overnight wonder, we were,' she'd smiled. 'Cathedral didn't burn down so they've pushed off.'

He had just started on his kedgeree when Nutkin appeared at the dining-room door, looked around pressingly, spotted him – and hurried over.

'Morning, Mr Chapter Clerk. Come to breakfast, have you? Help yourself over there.'

Despite his own urgent manner the invitation gave Nutkin pause – but not for food. 'Thank you, no, Mr Treasure,' he replied, forcing a brief smile to indicate that, while he could humour a whim as well as the next man, breakfast was not a meal a prominent member of the Litchester community could consider taking outside the marital home. 'Disturbing news, I'm afraid. Thought I should tell you without delay.'

'I'm sorry to hear it. Fire ahead. Coffee perhaps?'

From the tone Treasure sensed his consumption of *The Times* as well as his breakfast might be up for attenuation. He continued tucking into the peppered haddock while trying not to give the appearance of greed or to precipitate indigestion.

'Pounder may have died of head wounds. Most likely inflicted by . . .'

'The Dean's mace?'

'Possibly. May I ask how you knew that?'

'I didn't. There was something going on late last night, though. Renewed interest by indiscreet bevies of coppers at the cathedral.' He took a draught of coffee. 'If he was done in by a blunt instrument, the mace is pretty obviously the front runner.' He scooped up another forkful of kedgeree – and a fishbone with it.

'The formal post-mortem isn't till this morning. There'll be an official police statement after that. The superintendent in charge called me at midnight.' Nutkin paused for this earnest of his importance to register. Treasure, still busy with the bone, somewhat failed in the acknowledging. The lawyer made the sucking noise that preceded or punctuated a good many of his utterances. 'Terrible shock. Terrible. Difficult to comprehend.'

'Naturally.' The banker shook his head.

'It seems death occurred between six-fifteen and a quarter to seven. The likelihood of a burglar or a vandal being responsible is being examined.'

'But not very seriously?'

'I'm sorry?'

The banker wiped his mouth with his napkin. 'Uncomfortable as the thought may be – for all of us – the Magna Carta going up in flames on the night it did suggests deeper causes. Even sophisticated ones. Or don't you agree?'

'The thought has crossed my mind, certainly. Except that since murder may be indicated we are forced to the conclusion we are not looking at the work of some disaffected, not to say deranged member of our cathedral community. More likely a common thief. Surprised and resisted probably by a brave old man.'

'Daft thing to pinch. The Magna Carta,' was Treasure's immediate response to this appealingly lyrical but somehow over-convenient solution. 'I mean, how would a thief dispose of it once he'd got it?'

'One hears about unscrupulous London dealers. With international connections.' The lawyer paused, sucking in air. 'We cannot ignore that the offer of over a million pounds was known to a number of people. It put a new value, a new attraction on the item.'

'People here talked about the £1.1 million?'

'Not only people here, Mr Treasure.'

The banker took the point very quickly, as well as the possible reason for the early call and the mention of London dealers. 'How many people outside Litchester knew of the offer? Say, four weeks ago?'

'Officially? I imagine hardly any.'

'Officially only me?'

Nutkin's pale face took on a look of some embarrassment. 'That's possible. However . . .'

'I was told by you in a confidential letter which was seen only by me and my totally reliable secretary. I've mentioned the offer to one other person. The chairman of Grenwood, Phipps, just before the time last evening when your Mr Pounder got the chop. If there's been some sort of tip-off that caused a London gang to attempt a snatch, I think you'll have to look elsewhere for the source.' Treasure smiled expansively before re-applying himself to his kedgeree.

Now the lawyer looked distinctly uncomfortable. 'There's been a good deal of loose talk here. By people who should have known better. The news could easily have spread that way. Please don't think . . . by implying the miscreant could be from the outside I was . . .'

'Only pointing to the obvious,' Treasure cut in. 'Cathedral cities like this one don't usually harbour well-organised international crooks. Or even disorganised ones. I understand your point. Did you know the insurance cover on the Magna Carta had been increased to a million since the offer was formalised?'

Nutkin sucked in his cheeks for marginally longer than usual before replying. 'I don't believe I was aware of that. It wouldn't follow that I should have been told.' It was reasonably clear, however, that the speaker himself thought he should have been. 'Are you suggesting the insurance company leaked the information?'

'Certainly not.' Treasure paused with a coffee-cup halfway to his lips. 'The action just widens the number of people alerted to the increased value, that's all. People outside Litchester, too.' He drank the coffee. 'But I'd still guess what happened was done by a local. Could be whatever was intended went dreadfully wrong. Out of control. A lot of people might have been choosing to destroy the Magna Carta last night. People who'd never knowingly hurt a human being, let alone commit murder.'

'I don't follow, I'm afraid.'

'Take anyone who wanted the thing sold who thought it wouldn't be. Why not arrange for it to be burnt by accident? The cathedral gets a million in insurance. Almost as good as selling to the Americans.'

'The Dean and Canon Brastow have been promoting the sale. It's difficult to credit . . .'

'My dear chap, I didn't mean people at that level. Not necessarily anyway.' He sniffed. 'You said there'd been a lot of loose talk. Is there anyone of importance attached to the cathedral who hasn't taken sides? Anyone who didn't have a theory about how the voting would go this morning? I gather the fact the meeting's on and why is absolutely common knowledge.'

'You may be right. A relatively enclosed community like this one.' Nutkin shrugged. 'It's difficult to keep things secret for any length of time.'

'I gathered also last night that quite a few people were opposing the sale merely for conscientious reasons?'

'Not because they cared about the document itself, you mean? That may be true. I can't speak for any of them, naturally, but Canon Merit might come into that category. He and I have been of much the same view.'

'Not wanting the Charter to leave the country?'

'Exactly. Canon Jones was also opposed to selling on a matter of principle. We could all be said to have our attitudes reflected in those of other perhaps less . . . responsible people.'

'But any conscientious objector to a sale might have salved his conscience by staging a fire. Removing the morally difficult artefact and substituting the bland insurance money.'

'It seems far-fetched.'

'Of course.' And especially so, the banker construed, to a self-professed objector. 'So your money's on one of the sellers who thought my vote would block a sale?'

'We are speculating wildly, Mr Treasure,' Nutkin half-remonstrated, while giving the appearance of someone who rarely speculated at all, and never wildly. 'For my own part, I still believe Pounder's death was perpetrated by a callous criminal.'

'And I hope you're proved right. Incidentally, did you mention my voting intention to anyone?'

'More coffee, sir? Good morning, Mr Nutkin. Can I get you anything?' The motherly lady was standing by the table.

Nutkin regarded her for a moment, blinked, then gave her a cautious smile. 'Good morning, Mabel. Nothing for me, thank you.' He glanced at the time, then turned his head slowly towards Treasure, except his gaze had become strangely detached. It was focused over the banker's shoulder where it remained for several seconds while the rest of Nutkin remained unmoving.

Treasure looked behind him, searching the room. Apart from the motherly woman who was moving back to the buffet, the place was now entirely empty. The banker's own expression showed a touch of apprehension. 'Are you . . . ?'

'I fear I must leave you.' Nutkin blinked again several times as he spoke. 'A number of other urgent things to see to. At my office in East Street.'

'Is the Chapter meeting still on? Hardly seems any point.'

'I believe it must take place. The Dean could cancel it, of course. No doubt he'll inform us if he does. But time is short.' Nutkin was on his feet.

'So I can expect to see you again later?'

'Certainly. Yes. Goodbye for the present, Mr Treasure.' The

lawyer backed into an empty chair, regarded it testily, closed his eyes for a moment, then left with a determined expression if a less than determined step. Treasure watched him thoughtfully, then looked down at the now cold and, despite his best efforts, only half-consumed kedgeree.

'Some nice hot scrambled eggs and bacon instead, sir? I'll get it for you. There's plenty.'

He hesitated. 'Thank you . . . Mabel. Just a little perhaps. With a mushroom or two?' It really did pay to come down if you enjoyed a good breakfast.

'I'll be all right, love. I'm better now. Honest. I had a bit of sleep.' Nora Jakes, fifty-four and only daughter of the late Mr Pounder, poured herself another cup of tea. She was small, frail and usually breathless. Henry, her husband, was sitting across from her at the table in the kitchen of the small Victorian house they would now own. It was in a part of town where property had been cheap when her father had bought the place years before. It was not far from the cathedral, but on the other side of the river.

'Don't seem natural. Not after all those years,' said Jakes, staring at the seat normally occupied by his father-in-law.

'Wasn't natural. I know that now. Knew it from the start, too.'

'How d'you mean?'

'He'd never have knocked that heater over on his own. Even if he was taken ill. Had to be foul play. Thieves. It's terrible, the way things are today.'

'That's right.' He realised they'd been talking at cross-purposes – that she wasn't herself yet. It had been a shock, a double shock – first to learn her father had died, then four hours later to be told he'd likely been murdered. She wasn't strong: it was her heart, the doctor said, like her mother who'd died young.

'And how would they know if he was asleep? When he was hit?'

'It's only what they thought. That he could have been asleep. Or fainted. Expect they can find out things like that. At a post-mortem. He did sleep a lot, of course.' He'd finished cautiously.

'Only when he was off duty. Like at home. He wouldn't have dropped off when he was in charge of something. Not when he was in charge of the Old Library, surely?' But there was uncertainty in her voice.

'He was a very old man, love.'

'You mean if we're asked we ought to say he could have fallen asleep?' She caught her breath.

'And no disgrace in that. For someone his age. Not like being careless on purpose.'

'Better if he was asleep. In a way. For him, I mean. But why hit him at all in that case? Oh dear. Poor dad.' Her eyes had filled with tears again.

'No accounting for what a tearaway will do. When he found there was no money up there. Like as not he just turned to being malicious. Cruel and malicious for the sake of it. No other explanation. Like you said, doesn't have to be any these days.'

She dabbed her eyes and then her mouth with a screwed-up handkerchief. 'And it's not right anyone goes on thinking Dad did it without permission from someone.'

'Used the heater, you mean? I'll try to see the Dean again this morning. After I've been to the undertaker's.' He was even more determined than she was to get it clear – or clear enough – that the old man never did anything without a nod from the authorities. Law-abiding to a fault he'd been. If there was compensation money at stake – and Jakes thought there ought to be – it was risky having suspicion of bare negligence hanging about.

She sighed. 'Wish we knew when we can have the service. Doesn't seem reverent, having to wait.'

'Up to the coroner, then the police. That's what they told me.'

'Will they delay on the will, too?'

'Shouldn't think so,' he answered promptly. He was surprised but glad she'd asked the question. It wasn't a subject he could very well have raised – much as he'd wanted to. 'I'll go to the lawyer first thing if you like.' And the sooner the better was what he was thinking. They still had no clear idea how much the old man had stashed away in his box at the bank. They knew there was two thousand in the National Savings Bank passbook he'd kept at home.

'At least Commander Bliter gave you the day off.'

'Only because of the others there last night. Stuck-up bastard. Pretending to be the Lord High Everything he was. Good reason, too.'

'How d'you mean?'

'Making out it wasn't his place to know who was doing what all of the time.'

She shook her head. 'I still don't understand.'

'Your dad's paraffin heater. He was shifting the blame for that to Duggan.'

'But it wasn't Mr Duggan's heater.'

'No, and Duggan was making sure everybody knew it. Not his heater and not his responsibility. Bliter couldn't have known about it, either, though. That's what Duggan said. Like it was rehearsed. Something well below the Commander's range – oh, yes. Except it wasn't. Nor Duggan's either.'

'But Dad . . .'

'Duggan knew about the heater. So did Bliter. They were passing the buck, that's all. By rights they should have stopped Dad using it. Like I tried to unofficially. But they didn't. Because he could have refused to go on without. Would have meant someone else doing that last shift every day. One of the paid vergers. Like as not summer as well, once Dad got out of the habit.'

'So Mr Duggan just pretended he didn't know?'

'That's right. Saying your dad was a law to himself. And he'll get all the other vergers to back him. What's the betting money'll change hands over that?'

'That's terrible.'

'And it's not the worst.' Jakes had got very red in the face and for the moment seemed to have forgotten the tragedy of his father-in-law's death. 'Duggan's not getting money. Duggan's getting your dad's job. Bliter's said so.'

'But that was meant for you. Dad always said. Because the

Dean would see to it. When the time came. Oh, that's awful. You didn't tell me?'

'Didn't seem right to tell you. Not last night. Don't seem right now. All the same, now you know.' He seemed to be more in control of himself. 'I'll take it up with the Dean. As good as promised, it was. "Not suitable work for a gardener,"' he went on, with a not very good imitation of Percy Bliter. 'That's what he said to me. When we were all coming away last night. What he meant was he needed a bribe for Duggan. So he'd keep his mouth shut. Well, there's plenty can play at that game. Opening mouths as well as closing them,' he ended darkly.

# Chapter Eight

'Mr Treasure is it? I thought it must be. I'm . . . I'm Ursula Brastow.'

It seemed to have taken all her courage to present herself in this way. Her plump cheeks continued twitching irregularly as she stood beside the banker in the cathedral near the cloister door.

'Delighted to meet you. I met Canon Brastow last night. I say, isn't this tomb quite remarkable? Eight hundred years old.' He nodded enthusiastically at what he'd stopped to examine before she'd caught up with him, then turned to her again, smiling. 'I hope your husband won't have minded my slipping in for the tail end of the service.'

'Oh. I'm sure not. I'm quite sure.'

'I came over straight after breakfast. It was earlier than I'd imagined. And I'd quite forgotten there'd be an eight o'clock service. Expect there's one every morning.'

Canon Brastow had been the celebrant at the early communion that Treasure had found going on in the Lady Chapel beyond the High Altar. The banker's presence had increased the size of the congregation by a third.

'Every morning,' she repeated, then after taking a deep breath went on: 'I've been wondering what you could have thought about my—'

'And I'm Olive Merit. How's Molly?' interrupted the Chancellor's sister, who had just come up behind them and who had also been at the service.

Treasure looked pleased. 'So you know my wife?'

'Not seen her for donkey's years. School chums. That's all.'

'Well, she's fine. Filming at the moment. In America. I'll tell her we've met.'

'And give her my regards. Such a celebrity now.' But was the compliment a touch patronising? Perhaps so, he thought, as she went on. 'Sporting of you to thicken up our numbers at early service. Especially in a Protestant month.'

'I'm sorry?'

'Clive Brastow is Canon Residentiary in December. Ursula's husband. The Brastows represent the Low Church element in the close, don't you, Ursula?'

'I suppose you're right,' the other woman almost whispered. But she was evidently grateful that Olive Merit had acknowledged her existence.

'Not great communion-goers, the Prots aren't. Not much following for Clive and the Holy Eucharist. He packs 'em in at Sunday evensong, though. Powerful preacher. Makes the money-changers squirm. The bankers.' She fixed the Vice Chairman of Grenwood, Phipps with a lightly accusing grin.

'Canon Merit . . . ?'

'My brother.'

'I see. High churchman, of course.'

'Yes. Anglo-Catholic. Spiky as they come. Like the Dean. And Canon Jones. The wives, too. Clive Brastow never looks right in a chasuble. Like just now. Did you notice? My brother never looks right without one.' The last observation was punctuated by a disarming and reverberating snort.

'Sad business last night,' said Treasure.

'You know old Pounder was done in?' Miss Merit enquired. The three had begun walking towards the door.

'Mr Nutkin told me earlier.'

'Police kept us up till all hours. You, too, Ursula?'

'Quite late, Olive, yes.'

So much for Nutkin's confidential word from the superintendent, thought Treasure. Aloud he said: 'I'm waiting to hear if the Chapter meeting's still on.'

'The one you came for? It will be,' answered Miss Merit firmly.

'Dean's a stickler for keeping formal arrangements. Good chance you'll find a policeman in attendance, of course.' She made the snorting noise again but a very short one. 'Just your line, Mr Treasure. Weren't you involved in sudden death recently? In a hotel? Near Hereford?'

'Remotely, yes.'

Mrs Brastow looked apprehensive.

'Thought so,' Miss Merit affirmed. 'Read about it. D'you think this was a hit-and-run job? Or something more sinister? Verger-bashing by demented cleric perhaps?'

Olive Merit's hearty frankness seemed now to be thoroughly unnerving the other woman.

Treasure wasn't sure he was comfortable with it, either. 'I've no idea. Inexplicable really. Even the dimmest sort of common thief might have known there'd be no money up there.' He lifted the heavy latch and swung the huge door open. 'And the thing of greatest value burnt to a cinder like everything else. Makes no sense at all.'

'Oh, come, Mr Treasure. Makes a lot of sense to the people who wanted the Magna Carta sold but thought you'd stop their game,' Miss Merit announced loudly as she marched through the door.

'Not all of them, Olive,' piped Ursula earnestly while scuffling along behind her.

'Oh, don't be a goose, Urs. I don't mean you or Clive. Hey, aren't we waiting for Clive? Ah, here he is. Confounded nuisance having to come this way. Wrong side of the building for all of us.'

Treasure had been about to close the door when Canon Brastow appeared, hurrying across the transept from the south choir aisle and buttoning his overcoat. 'Good morning, Mr Treasure. Glad to see you at the service.'

'Only half of it, I'm afraid. Your throat sounds better, Canon.'

'Much, thank you.'

'Don't you think the murderer could have been someone who wanted the Charter sold? Someone who thought it wouldn't be,

Clive? Because of Mr Treasure? Someone going for the insurance money?'

'Really Olive, that's a wholly irresponsible conjecture. A man is dead.'

'And that's a wholly pompous answer, almost worthy of my brother. People die all the time. In any case, our murderer wasn't out for himself. The cathedral gets the money whichever way you look at it.'

'It was still murder, or so we are led to believe. Something which cannot be condoned. Not in any circumstances. Not by responsible people.' It seemed Brastow and Miss Merit were quite at ease as conversational belligerents.

'Not even murder by mistake? It could happen. Ask Mr Treasure. He's an expert.'

Brastow looked from Olive to the banker in some surprise.

'Nothing of the sort, I'm afraid. And I do wish my voting intentions weren't seen as affecting what's happened,' Treasure offered pointedly.

The group was outside now, beyond the cloister and on the pathway that led around to the east end of the cathedral. Three of the participants were walking abreast, with Ursula Brastow trailing and attempting to open a fold-up umbrella because a light drizzle had started. It was still not fully daylight.

'But in a positive way your voting intentions did let the non-sellers off the hook,' Miss Merit persisted. 'My brother and Miles Nutkin, for instance. Ewart Jones as well.' She buttoned the collar of her coat.

'That's not quite true. I told Nutkin on the phone yesterday I'd changed my mind.'

'You intended voting for the sale?' This was Clive Brastow.

'Mm. But I've yet to be persuaded that had any bearing on Pounder's death. There was nothing confidential about it. I don't know if Nutkin told anyone else. I meant to ask him.' Thinking back, he recalled he had asked him.

Ursula Brastow had the umbrella up. One of its struts was broken so that two limp brown panels hung down in front of her.

She was peering worriedly from around them, and made as if to speak but no one noticed.

'Doesn't affect my premise,' Miss Merit put in. 'Not in practice. Non-sellers wouldn't have gone to the stake to stop the sale. Or, more accurately, put old Pounder to the stake to stop it.'

Mrs Brastow hurried to come abreast of the others. 'Really, Olive,' Brastow remonstrated. 'You do choose the most . . .'

'You were going to vote for selling the Magna Carta, Mr Treasure? For selling? After all?' The interruption was so unexpected and the tone so loud and incredulous the others looked around in surprise.

'Yes. Changed my mind, I'm afraid, Mrs Brastow. After a great deal of thought. A very great deal,' Treasure added while regarding her with increasing embarrassment. 'I'm sorry, I meant . . .'

'Morning, all,' a breathless voice sounded from behind. It was Donald Welt in a track-suit with a towel about his neck. He was marking time at the double. 'Spiritually uplifted, are we? That's good. Morning, Mr Treasure.' He and the banker had met briefly the night before.

'Been praying for your immortal soul, Dr Welt,' Olive Merit observed tartly, 'but without any lively hope of success.'

'That's not original, Miss Merit,' puffed the bearded organist with matching acerbity. He was still running on the spot. 'Do better to pray for Ewart Jones. He may need it. Coppers arriving at his house when I was passing. Third degree, I should think. Well, mustn't get cold. See you in church.' He made off chuckling towards the cloisters, but leaving at least one of his hearers with a new concern.


Detective Chief Inspector Pride wasn't enjoying the interview, and a good deal less than the young detective constable seated in the corner of Canon Jones's study making notes. It wasn't the constable who was having metaphorically to tread on eggs without breaking shells.

At nearly fifty, Pride was not young for his rank, nor had he been at the time of the promotion. He had come by that last advancement – and previous ones – in the plodding, hardest way. Heavily built, over-weight, and normally a chain smoker, he had twice reached for his cigarettes in the last few minutes and both times stopped short of taking out the packet. Asking permission to light up and then filling the room with smoke would still further have reduced his narrow margin of moral advantage in the situation.

'So to be quite clear, sir, from what you've said, you went to the cathedral twice for the same purpose?'

'That's right, Mr Pride,' beamed the diminutive New Zealander from behind his desk. 'By the way, smoke if you like. Sorry I've given up keeping gaspers on offer. They go stale.'

The Chief Inspector shook his head, an action that reflected stoic self-discipline, and exercised his wide bullfrog jowls. 'You didn't mention the first visit. Not when you were questioned last night, sir.' He spoke slowly, through almost closed lips, and seemed to choose his words with hesitation.

'I could say nobody asked me, Mr Pride.' The speaker held up his hand to forestall a reply. 'But I won't. Fact is I wasn't exactly *compos mentis* last night. Consequence of falling arse over elbow down those steps.'

The constable in the corner looked up briefly, exchanged grins with Canon Jones, and went back to his notes.

'I see, sir,' said Pride, shifting in his chair. 'So on the first visit, at approximately ten past six, you entered through the north door.'

'That's right. Risky. I might have been seen. But quick and easy because that door's usually still open then. I had my key if it wasn't of course. The Old Library's supposed to be closed before that.'

'But it wasn't? You went up the west-turret stairs. The door was shut and the key was in the lock.'

'Showing Mr Pounder was still inside.'

'You didn't lock the door and take the key, sir?'

'Certainly not.'

'But you went away without going in?'

The Canon leant forward, nodding. 'Didn't suit my daring purpose.'

'Which you say was to take away the Magna Carta. Take it away secretly and unofficially, sir?'

'I think "quietly purloin" would about fit the case.'

'And this was again what you intended to do on the second visit?'

'Too right. Pity I hadn't tried it the first time.' He paused. 'Might have saved old Pounder's life. Poor devil. Would have been too late the second time of course, since he was dead by quarter to seven.'

The Chief Inspector cleared his throat. 'And you'd have kept the Magna Carta hidden until an appeal was launched? To raise three million pounds for the cathedral?'

'A lot more than we'd have got from selling it.'

'That was to be the er . . . the ransom, sir?'

'For the good of the people of the diocese and the country to focus on. To bring them to realising the extent of the responsibility. The one we'd be abrogating with a sale. Would have been the end of that caper, I guarantee. Force of public opinion.'

'How er . . . how was everyone to know about this, sir? About it being ransomed?'

'Anonymous calls to the *Daily Express* and the BBC.' The answer came very promptly. 'That would have done it, don't you think?'

Pride frowned but didn't comment.

'It would also have spelled out the Charter was safe,' the Canon added.

'Provided the money was raised, sir?'

'Provided the appeal was started. Which it would have been. I'd have returned the Charter after that. After the publicity. When the point had been made. The sale stopped.' He gave a satisfied grin.

'I see, sir.'

'People would have come to understand that even after flogging a treasure we'd still have had to raise another two million.'

'You didn't think of it as . . . as a highly irregular operation, sir?'

The Canon bounced twice on his seat. 'My dear chap, of course I did. That was the whole idea. How else d'you wake people up these days? But it wouldn't have harmed anybody.'

'Would have involved a serious police investigation, sir, as like as not.'

'Not, I'd say.'

The policeman blinked.

'Look, Mr Pride, as a young man, at university, I was involved in rags a lot scarier than this one. All aimed at raising money for good causes. The police never took them seriously.'

'That would have been in New Zealand, sir?' Worse than British universities by the sound of it.

'Sure. But you have them in this country, too. Plenty. What's the difference? Everyone would have known this was a jape with a happy ending. Assumed it was being handled by responsible people.'

'There were others involved, sir?'

'No, there weren't. I was speaking loosely. It was an impulse idea. Came to me yesterday morning. When I was trying to find an angle for the cathedral appeal. Something to attract more money and attention then we'd get by selling the Magna Carta. Confiscating it seemed spot on. Still does.'

Repentant if sinful clergymen were not entirely outside Pride's professional experience, though he'd never had to deal with one above the parish level. An unrepentant but confessedly sinful clergyman was quite new to him at any level. He half-closed his eyes, which always helped him clear his thoughts.

'And you'd have got at the Magna Carta by opening the display cabinet with a key, sir?'

'The common spare key. Kept on the locked keyboard in the Chapter House. All the canons have a key to that. I simply . . . borrowed the cabinet key after the Chapter meeting yesterday afternoon. I still have it.' He searched in his pocket, then produced the object.

'And the key to the old Library, sir?'

'Got that the same way. From the Chapter House keyboard. Fits the west-turret door. I believe you have that one, Mr Pride?'

'That's right, sir. Taken from the lock after the fire.' The Chief Inspector considered matters for a moment.

'Wouldn't people have known where the keys had come from? After the . . . purloining?'

'Not at all. The locks might have been picked. Or duplicate keys used. I was aiming to put back the ones I used after dinner last night.'

'You had a key to the Chapter House, sir?'

'Certainly. All Chapter members do.'

'You were overlooking we'd have interviewed everybody with keys or access to them?'

'Probably, Mr Pride.' This came with an expansive smile. 'You're suggesting I hadn't thought that part through well enough? I'm sure you're right. I told you it was all done on impulse. In the end people would have known who'd taken the Charter, of course.'

'Why, sir?'

'Because I'd have told them, naturally. After I'd put it back. That would only have been right and fair, don't you think? In case others were suspected.'

'Yes, sir. I'd certainly think that.' There was more than a hint of indulgence in the tone. He glanced across at the constable, who looked back knowingly for no reason other than he thought it was expected of him. 'So we've established the reason for your visits to the cathedral last evening, sir. And you're sure you didn't see anyone else at either time, sir?'

'Quite sure. As I said, I only wish I'd had the sense to go in and see what Pounder was doing.'

'You seem certain he was in the Old Library on your first visit, sir?'

The Canon looked surprised. 'Positive, Mr Pride.' He pushed back his chair. 'Knew his habits. He left the keys in the locks when he arrived. Took them out when he left.'

'Except he normally locked up at six.'

'Which should have made me think he might have been ill.'

'But you didn't smell fire, sir?'

'Not till the second time. When I was getting the door open.'

Now he had risen and was pacing in front of the window behind his desk, a few steps in each direction. He had thrust his thumbs into his waistcoat pockets. 'If there'd been burning the first time, you'd think I'd have smelled it?' He shook his head. 'The second time, at the start, I kept telling myself Pounder had left. Locked up. Because his key had gone.'

'But you said the door wasn't locked, sir.'

Jones stopped pacing. One hand went to his creased forehead. 'I may have been confused, Mr Pride. Could be I still am. The key was gone certainly. I remember fitting the one I'd brought. I might have turned it in the lock. Could have done. That was before I remembered the wretched door opened outwards. And when I lifted the latch it did. With a vengeance.'

'And you're positive you didn't go in the first time, sir?' Pride asked especially slowly.

For the first time the little clergyman showed irritation. 'Of course I'm positive. I'm not senile.'

Pride got up to leave, nodded to the constable and reached for his cigarettes. 'You did say you might be confused, sir. Still.'

# Chapter Nine

'The New Library's over there, Mr Treasure, at the end of the cloister. That's the start of the Bishop's Palace beyond. And thanks again for the advice. And for promising to protect my dad from the cops.' Glynis Jones finished with an elfin smile. She drew up the Suzuki on the left in Bridge Street, in front of the cathedral. 'You don't think Dad should ask to know who saw him going in the cathedral? The first time?'

Treasure opened the door to get out – and to leave the front passenger-seat vacant for Jingles. The little terrier was already anticipating this promotion in a frenzy of activity in the back.

'Not much point really. And I think the policeman's only doing his job, you know? Of course, your father really needs protecting from himself.' He paused, pouting. 'It was the most extraordinary admission to make when he didn't need to make any.'

'My dad's a pretty extraordinary man. He's not unworldly. Just disarmingly honest.'

Proving, Treasure considered inwardly, that too much virtue can be quite as dangerous as too little in a cynical world. Aloud he said, 'I'll do anything I can. But I don't believe you or your mother should worry unduly.'

'Dad won't, that's for sure. So somebody has to. See you for lunch, then. After I've paid my farmworkers. Thanks again. You're a sport.'

Pulling up the collar of his sheepskin, the banker watched the little vehicle speed off towards the ancient stone bridge. It was nine-thirty and still drizzling.

Ten minutes earlier the girl had sought him out at the hotel.

She had told him about Canon Jones's interview with the police – which had ended in the cleric being asked somewhat ominously not to leave the town without telling them. She was disturbed that when her father had given his account of what had been said he had been blissfully unconcerned that he might have put himself under suspicion. She had come to Treasure for advice because she and her mother didn't want to approach anyone else – at least not yet.

So, as counsellor by default, the banker had tried to steer a middle course. Presumably Canon Jones, who he had yet to meet, was innocent of anything worse than impulsive, daring intentions and equally impulsive and daring admissions. The police would balance both with the fact they were dealing with a clerical luminary unlikely to be indictable on more counts than the ones he had voluntarily introduced.

Or might such wholesome admissions add up to a disingenuous ploy on the Canon's part?

Treasure debated the last proposition while following one of the paths that dissected the wide grassed area separating Bridge Street from the west end of the cathedral and its flanking satellite buildings. These last ran away to the south, the New Library being the furthest of them. It was evidently modern but decently compatible with the twelfth-century cloister to which it was joined.

Like the Old Library the new one had two storeys, but with an enclosed ground floor. It was an oblong, plain stone building with an Italianate flavour and about half as big again as its recently damaged predecessor. Treasure was encouraged to see the inside lights were on. The main doorway, set back under a round arch, was at the near end of the elevation he was approaching. He had been about to try the door when it opened.

'You're supposed to ring,' said the advancing young clergyman, who was zipping up a hooded rain-jacket. But he hesitated before pulling the door shut behind him.

'Then, I'll do just that,' replied the banker. 'It's Minor Canon Twist, isn't it? My name's Treasure. We met last night. With Miss Purse. I'm here hoping to see her.'

'Oh, sorry.' Twist pushed the blond hair off his forehead. 'Come in, please. Didn't recognise you. Too much on my mind.' He stepped back, and Treasure followed him into a glass-walled vestibule.

'Still involved over the fire, I expect,' said the banker.

'No. Freshly involved over the murder,' the other replied solemnly. 'Police have been on to all the cloister residents. Checking on where people were between six-fifteen and a quarter to seven last night. Who they were with. Who they saw.'

'And you were able to account for yourself?'

'He was with me.' It was Laura Purse who answered. She had appeared from inside the library. 'Good morning, Mr Treasure. Did you sleep well?'

'Yes, thanks. So you're both suitably alibi'd?' He smiled. 'But I doubt you're suspects.'

'You don't know,' cut in Twist. 'Very officious the police are.' He turned to Laura. 'And we weren't together the whole time.'

'Yes, we were. In my flat. For as long as makes no matter. I noticed the time, Gerard. You didn't. Remember?' Her tone was more instructive than insistent.

'Except I've told the police . . .'

'And we've agreed you're going to untell them. If necessary.' She moved a hand across her hair, which she wore tight to her head and dramatically swept back in a bun. 'Don't you have a class to take?'

'Heavens, yes. I'm late. See you.' He looked from one to the other, gave a half-hearted grin, then left hurriedly.

'And what can I do for you, Mr Treasure?' Her words continued measured and unruffled. She motioned him past a staircase and through the unframed glass door into the room lined and sprigged with tall, matching wooden bookcases. This evidently comprised the rest of the ground floor. The librarian's desk, computer workstation and filing cabinets were arranged near the door and forward of the first set of bookcase sprigs. There was a long double-sided reading desk in the central corridor running the length of the room, but the place had the appearance of being primarily one person's domain.

'You can spare me a few minutes?'

'Delighted. Do sit down.' She picked some fluff from the shoulder of the tight-fitting black sweater. 'Poor Gerard. Such a lamb, but sheltered. Needs protecting by us worldly ones.'

It seemed this was an occupational requirement amongst the Litchester Cathedral clergy but, Treasure concluded, one with which Gerard Twist, at least, was well provided.

The banker was not displeased to be rated one of the cavalier kind, and on so short an acquaintance. 'There's no reason surely why anyone should think he's involved in Pounder's death?'

'Of course not,' she answered dismissively. 'I believe the police are trying to link the death with the pending sale of the Magna Carta. Which suggests to them any of the cathedral people might have been mixed up in it. Pretty farfetched, I'd have thought.'

'But you were together over the critical period?'

'Mm. Gerard wasn't quite sure of times. He never is. We were listening to Bach. How's that for innocent diversion?'

'Immaculate, I'd think.' Certainly he rated the almond-eyed Laura Purse as diverting. 'So, of course, he couldn't have seen anyone else, either?'

'That's right,' she answered shortly in a manner which suggested an end to the subject.

He looked about him. 'You're the sole librarian?'

'Librarian and archivist, yes. With graduate students helping in the long vacation.'

'You get a lot of readers?'

'No, but the quality's superb.' She smiled. 'A lot of dons from overseas universities. Readers' tickets are issued strictly on recommendation. It's an expensive collection. So's the maintenance.'

'Who does the paying? The cathedral?'

'The Dean and Chapter pay for a bit of me. But I come mostly courtesy of a charitable grant.' She paused, then, in answer to his quizzical look, added, 'The Cheviot Educational Foundation.'

'Interesting. I don't know it. American, I suppose?'

'Anglo-American. The readers and the summer students are mostly from the States.'

'And the grant's renewed annually?'

'Every three years. To provide the unworthy holder with peace of mind.' She gave a deprecating smile. 'It also allows for worthwhile application. Primarily on the compiling of complicated indexes. On the location and nature of Christian manuscripts. Especially those housed outside universities.'

'Such as the ones wiped out last night?'

She shook her head. 'All seventeenth-century copies. Mostly incomplete, and mostly made from originals we keep here, upstairs. Still, it was a pity to lose them.'

'And they're lost completely, I gather.'

'Utterly. They let me into the Old Library last night. And again this morning. Under heavy police escort.' She squeezed her shoulders inwards in a graceful gesture of resignation. 'The only bits of the chained library left are the chains. The bookcase burnt as thoroughly as the books.'

'Same goes for the Magna Carta and its case.'

'Afraid so. Much more awful, though. The Charter was worth so much.'

'The manuscript books – the copies – they weren't valuable?'

'Weren't insured for much. They were there simply to give visitors an impression of a chain library. And how it worked. The bookcase was a good reconstruction.'

'You said the books were seventeenth-century.'

'There was a scriptorium here between 1620 and 1636.'

'A scriptorium being?'

'Sorry, a place where they copy manuscripts.'

'But this was long after the invention of printing.'

'And long before the invention of the typewriter.'

'You mean they were copying letters? That kind of thing?'

'Yes. And illuminated scrolls. And some books. The Litchester scriptorium was special. Bigger than you'd expect because they taught as well as practised manuscript illumination and decoration.

The bishop at the time objected to the way printing had debased calligraphy.'

'Wasn't he fighting a losing battle?'

'In a way. You could say he was an early conservationist. He got support from a few county bigwigs. But the scriptorium didn't pay. Plenty of pupils. Not enough work. To keep the students occupied they set them to copying the big manuscript works in the library. Like the Gospels.'

'Which must have taken years to do.'

'Not with teams of apprentices involved. But it's why the results were patchy in quality, and sometimes incomplete. Like the copies we lost last night.'

'Pity that Magna Carta wasn't a copy,' Treasure grunted.

'It wasn't, I'm afraid. It was last authenticated by experts, let's see . . .' She reached for a file, flipped over some pages, and traced down another with a slim, well-manicured hand. 'Yes, just over four years ago. No copy, and I wouldn't know where to look for one. We don't have one here.' The last comment was especially assertive.

'Mr Pounder seems to have thought there were some.'

'Really? That's news to me. Pounder was a romantic.' She grinned. 'And, to prove it, he was an indefatigable bottom-pincher. To the very last.'

'You don't say? Tarnishes the stainless reputation.'

'He was harmless. Probably got the idea of Magna Carta copies from the scriptorium collection here. A load of loyal addresses to the King and others from nobles and bishops and lord mayors. Some of those were duplicated. But they all date from the time of James I and Charles I.'

'Sounds fascinating.'

'Like to see? Upstairs.'

It was partly what he'd come for – that and the information she had given him already. The following half-hour he found wholly absorbing.

The upper floor housed a half-partitioned binding room and, in the bigger area, bookcases for venerable large volumes, and chests of slim metal display-drawers – the permanent repositories for the collection of parchment scrolls. After showing Treasure how to use the index and the drawers, which were hinged and removable, Miss Purse had returned to her own work, leaving him to make his own selections.

'The County Sheriff in 1632 was a Colonel Michael d'Aras,' he remarked later downstairs, as he was taking his leave. 'Name mean anything?'

'Yes,' Laura answered smiling. 'He pops up in a lot of the scrolls. Not surprising in view of his office. If you were petitioning the King, or even the Bishop, for a favour of some kind . . .'

'It made sense to have the County Sheriff's name on your formal plea. I see. He'd be one of the county bigwigs you mentioned?'

'Who supported the scriptorium? I expect so. Why the interest?'

'The coincidence of the name with something else. D'you suppose there's still a d'Aras family living locally? The name could have been anglicised, of course. But there's no d'Aras or Daras in there. I've looked.' He nodded at the telephone directory which she had pulled out and had already started to leaf through.

She closed the directory. 'Then, I suppose that's the answer to your question. I've never heard of a contemporary d'Aras.'

'No matter. I must go. Thanks again.'

He left the library and headed for the Chapter House still debating an inconsistency. Surely the apprentices at the under-used scriptorium must have been put to copying the Litchester Magna Carta? And, if that were so, why had no copies survived? The library was over-endowed with originals and replicas of many documents that could only have been of passing interest at any time; yet the Great Charter must have had a huge attraction for every generation.

'Excuse me, sir?' The small, stoutish man raised his bowler hat. 'Did I see you leaving the cathedral library?'

'That's right.'

'I'm a visitor, you understand?' He fingered the top button of the worn, russet-coloured Raglan-style topcoat.

'So am I. We arrived on the same train last night. And I believe we both breakfasted at the Red Dragon this morning.' The banker smiled affably.

'You're very observant, sir. Very.' The obsequious approach entirely matched the character. 'Imagine you noticing me?' The man winked his left eye – twice. 'I was wondering. Could you tell me? How do you get permission to use the library?' He winked again: the action seemed to be involuntary.

'I get it because I have a formal connection with the cathedral.' This didn't seem an exaggeration coming from the vicar's warden of Great St Agnes. 'Normally, I understand, one needs a recommendation from a place of learning. You're researching something?' The middle-aged enquirer looked an unlikely academic but appearances often deceived.

'You might say that, yes. Researching. I'm actively engaged on important research.' He weighed the words, giving the impression Treasure's speculation while new to him had proved wholly apposite. Next he glanced questioningly to both sides as if to gauge the effect of what he'd said upon others – except there was no one close enough to have heard him.

'Then I suggest you ring the bell and speak with the librarian.'

'You do? How kind.' But instead of moving off to the library the man fell into step with Treasure, who was going in the opposite direction. 'Terrible thing, the fire last night. I'd been hoping to visit the chained library.'

Which was not, of itself, confirmation of higher intellectual endeavour, the banker thought. 'Only second-rate copies of manuscript books there, of course,' he said. 'Unless . . .'

'The Magna Carta.' The man winked again. 'That's different. A serious loss.'

'To the nation.' The other closed both eyes and blew his nose very loudly in a red check handkerchief. 'You know they were going to sell it?'

'It wasn't certain.' And he should know, though he questioned why he should be debating the point with a total stranger.

'It was in the paper. That they were selling. Didn't state how much. They're saying now there was murder as well as the fire.' The man gave a low whistle. 'Well, there's a bobby-dazzler if you like,' he said, entirely changing the subject. His last comment had been about the red-haired young woman in the short skirt who had just overtaken them – and loud enough for her to hear. Cindy Larks glanced over her shoulder and smiled enquiringly – at Treasure. The other man had stopped, but not to get a better view of the girl. His interest in her seemed to have waned as promptly as it had surfaced: he was searching for something in several pockets.

The banker could now hardly follow his inclination to hurry on alone and rid himself of an embarrassing hanger-on – not without appearing to be chasing after the girl. Compromising, he turned off the path and strode out across the grass – past a notice that requested people not to.

'Sorry about that. Weakness of mine. The bird, I mean. The name's Hawker. Mine, not hers.' He was moving again at Treasure's side, half-running to keep up, and still digging into his pockets. 'Len Hawker. Of Hawker & Bowles. Bowles is dead now. Very painful. And inconvenient, as it happened. Still.' He was wheezing loudly. 'Sure I've got a card here somewhere.'

'Well, goodbye, Mr Hawker.'

'Just one other point, Mr Treasure.'

Now it was Treasure who stopped, staring down testily, though not because he was incensed or even interested in why this fellow had troubled to find out his name – presumably at the hotel. 'Look, I'm due at the Chapter House. For a meeting. If . . .'

'The Chapter House is over there. You're going in the wrong . . .'

'Direction. I know that. Will you kindly . . .'

'I've heard the price was £1.1 million. For the Magna Carta. Will you confirm that, Mr Treasure?'

'Certainly not.'

'But you don't deny it?'

'I shall certainly deny answering your question. What is it you do, anyway? What do Hawker & Bowles do?'

'Corporate enquiries, Mr Treasure. Personal ones, too, should you ever feel the need. Short-handed at the moment. Owing to bereavement.'

'And which corporation are you enquiring for?'

Hawker looked genuinely surprised. 'That would have to be confidential, sir.' He paused and gave a long wink. 'Tell you this, though. For nothing.' He winked again, moving closer to the banker, who yielded slightly before a leeward whiff of tobacco-laden breath. 'We've got an interest in common. Oh, yes. Can't say more, you understand?'

# Chapter Ten

'Nobody can say Ewart Jones shirked telling the truth.'

Canon Algy Merit was wresting virtue out of doleful and dire necessity.

There was a murmur of agreement from most of those sitting at the oblong oak table in the panelled Chapter meeting room.

'Plenty will say Ewart Jones is a bloody fool, of course. They're probably saying it already. Fact is, my friends, I'd made my . . . my disclosure before we knew there'd been a murder.' The New Zealander looked round at the others, his mouth pursed, his eyebrows raised.

'No doubt you'd have done the same afterwards, Ewart,' said the Dean without making it totally clear whether the remark was meant as a compliment.

'I hope so, Dean. Difficult to say.'

Treasure found Canon Jones's capacity for honesty and self-doubt commendable. It was difficult to be sure, though, that the sentiment was being reflected in the reactions of all those present.

The special Chapter meeting had taken only a few minutes. Speaking as chairman, and seated at the head of the table, the Dean had deplored the circumstance that had negated the purpose of the gathering, thanked Treasure for coming, asked for any other relevant business and, since there had been none, closed the formal proceedings with a prayer. He had then sat down again and enjoined a general, informal appraisal of events the night before and their likely consequences. Treasure had made to leave, but the Dean had specifically pressed him to stay.

'It would be sensible if we kept the doubt the Precentor's just expressed entirely to ourselves,' said Canon Brastow throatily, and staring fixed-necked at Canon Jones, who was on the opposite side of the table.

'In the Precentor's own interest,' Nutkin volunteered.

'In the interest of prudence. And to avoid further reflection on the way the Chapter handles its responsibilities.' With this, Brastow had firmly declined the proffered softener.

'You believe there's been a reflection on us as a responsible body, Clive?' the Dean turned his head in Brastow's direction. 'Good or bad?' he finished with a mischievous grimace.

'I should have thought that was obvious, Dean.' Brastow did his best to clear his throat. 'As if a murder hanging over our community wasn't enough, for the Precentor to have volunteered he intended stealing the Magna Carta last evening was, to say the least, ill-advised. But it would still be better to live with the consequences rather than equivocate.'

'Not steal? Temporarily remove into safe-keeping, I understood. Ewart?' questioned the Dean lightly but firmly.

'That was my intention, Dean.'

'And a great pity it wasn't fulfilled,' Treasure offered breezily, not sure if it was appropriate for him to speak at all, but remembering his promise to Glynis Jones. 'If Canon Jones had succeeded in removing the Magna Carta, I'm sure we'd all have been grateful.'

'That must be conjecture,' Brastow observed flatly, and causing a stir around the table. 'We don't know what circumstances might have applied.'

'We know Ewart raised the alarm and saved the cathedral.' This was Merit making virtues again.

'A fact that will be overshadowed – indeed, has already been overshadowed – by another one. Wholly uncommendable and quite lurid.'

'Clive, I think that's going too far. A lot too far,' the Dean put in quietly.

'No, it's fair comment,' said Canon Jones. 'The Treasurer

wouldn't have approved of my plan even if it'd gone without a hitch. Would you, Clive?'

'Far from just disapproving of it, I'd have said you'd taken leave of your senses,' Brastow obliged with feeling. 'Ignoring the tragic outcome, Ewart, how can you begin to justify what you had in mind? It was . . .' He hesitated, then swallowed with difficulty before going on. 'Forgive me, but it was juvenile and irresponsible. In the extreme. What can you possibly have expected it to achieve?'

'That's easy. A million pounds minimum. Hopefully three. An acceptance of its inherited obligations by this august body.'

'You mean this Chapter?'

'Too right I do. And finally a short sharp shaking to the core of the ecclesiastical establishment in this cathedral, this city, this diocese, and maybe even this country. But mostly this cathedral city. This quiet complacent backwater that's so drawn in on itself, so determined to protect itself from vulgar intrusions, it's forgotten why God put it here. Forgotten why generations of good Christian folk devoted their work, their fortunes and their lives so we could carry on promoting the Christian message in our turn with the same sacrifice and dedication. And that doesn't mean selling the flaming assets, because that's stealing for certain.'

'Thank you, Ewart, I'm sure that was good for all our souls,' the Dean broke the awkward silence that had followed the New Zealander's impassioned but still measured outburst. 'Also our sense of responsibility.'

'Personally I find Canon Jones's point of view very persuasive,' offered Treasure.

'Does that tell us how you'd have finally voted, Mr Treasure?' Algy Merit, seated beside Jones, lifted his gaze slowly from the centre of the table to study the banker opposite. 'I'd gathered you'd changed your mind. That you were in favour of selling. Might you have changed it again?'

'Since I came all the way to attend the meeting you can certainly assume I'd have listened to the arguments.' Treasure shrugged. 'I'm only sorry they've become academic.'

'Our sense of responsibility as perceived by the public is

anything but academic,' complained Brastow. 'And might I remind everyone that my house is far from being protected from vulgar intrusion? It's a refuge for those in need – hungry and unwashed.'

'Don't know how you do it,' said Algy Merit, shaking his head. 'Our boiler scarcely manages hot baths for the two of us.'

'Where there's a will,' rejoined the other icily. 'My point is, Ewart's confessed intention has made our sense of responsibility a subject for public derision.'

'Not our collective sense. Only Ewart's,' was Merit's serious rejoinder.

'And with any luck, Algy, they could write me off as a clerical error,' joked Ewart Jones.

'Where, for instance, do we stand in the matter of the paraffin heater?' asked Clive Brastow, unimpressed by the Precentor's levity.

'Pounder had no official authorisation for his heater,' Bliter came in quickly.

'Which is rather different from saying he used it without anyone's knowledge,' said Merit carefully, smoothing the purple edging of his cape. He and the Dean were the only ones present wearing cassocks.

'I suspected he was using it. Thought I smelled it last week. I've told the police as much.' The Dean's words produced no surprised looks – only some glum expressions. He smiled before continuing. 'Hope that solves a problem for anyone else who knew what the old boy was doing. Or guessed it. Better if I carry the can on that one.'

Bliter reddened and tugged at his shirt collar. 'Um . . . ,' he began uncertainly.

Nutkin shut him up with: 'That's very unselfish, Dean.'

'He was my verger after all.'

'Will it alter the attitude of the insurance company?' asked Merit. 'Will it stop them paying up?' He was heading off any burgeoning comment from Brastow that the Dean's admission would further confirm the public's alleged view of the Chapter's cupidity.

'The Dean asked me that. I don't think so,' Treasure volunteered with marginally more conviction than he felt was strictly justified.

His faith in the probity of godly men had taken several turns for the better since the start of his visit to Litchester. Where he stood on their sense of prudence was another matter. Indeed, if anyone present now confessed to somehow justified homicide he wouldn't have been one bit surprised. Meantime he was glad to throw in something positive as witness to the integrity of Mammon.

'The Administrator let me have the policy to look at before the meeting. I have it here,' the banker continued with a glance at Bliter. He opened the document in front of him. 'Whether any of Pounder's superiors knew he was using the heater I don't think is relevant. I understand at the time of his death he was working as a volunteer for no reward or other consideration.'

'Except his place in heaven,' Ewart Jones put in with conviction.

'What you mean is he wasn't acting as an employee under discipline? That he was a free agent?' questioned the Dean.

'That's roughly it. As I see it, he was entitled, as it were, to cause an accident. Just like any other visitor to the cathedral.'

'And the cathedral authorities will be entitled to claim compensation for the damage?' This was Clive Brastow, mindful of his office as Treasurer, and with relief sounding in every syllable.

Treasure nodded. 'That's whether Pounder started the fire by accident, or whether it was started by his murderer, obviously with criminal intent. Of course, that'll be up to the police or a jury to decide. But in either event I believe you'll be compensated.'

'Mr Treasure is chairman of the Regal Sun Assurance Company,' offered Bliter with due deference.

'So I'm relieved this policy is not with that company,' Treasure added glibly. He omitted to say that if it had been he wouldn't have been offering glad-handed opinions with nearly so much enthusiasm – if at all. There were limits.

'That being the only reassuring thing we've heard this morning, I suggest it earns a reward,' said the Dean. 'Something in any case that may appropriately be passed over to the vicar's warden of the Church of Great St Agnes.' He withdrew something wrapped in tissue from the pocket of his cassock. 'Compensation for troubling to come here. Can you all see?' He opened out the wrapping.

'Small piece of flat black stone, is it?' asked Algy Merit, leaning forward and stretching his short but ample neck.

'Much better than that,' said the Dean. 'It's believed to be all that's left of the Litchester Magna Carta. Not the parchment, I'm afraid. That was quite consumed. It's wax. Assumed to be from the seal. It melted, of course, but later reconstituted itself in a small hollow in one of the flagstones. Mr Olley, the head fireman, brought it to me this morning. The officials have no further use for it.' He pushed the fragment towards Treasure, who was seated on his right.

'I'm very grateful,' said the banker out of good manners but not immediately sure what he would do with the thing. He coughed. 'Perhaps I can have it mounted in some way.'

The middle-aged woman who had just come in had waited for Treasure to finish before she touched the Dean's sleeve, then whispered something to him.

The Dean frowned. 'It seems Detective Chief Inspector Pride is outside. Wants a word with some of us. Suppose we'd better break up.'

'Why not ask him in here, Dean?' suggested Canon Jones, adding with an expansive grin, 'I think I'd rather have him grill me again with all my legal and moral advisers present.'

It would hardly have been appropriate for this overt disclosing tactic by the Precentor to be resisted by anyone else, which is why the Detective Chief Inspector shortly found himself effectively co-opted to the Chapter table – feeling especially alone and conspicuous in a chair at the unoccupied end.

'. . . have to follow up on individuals known to have been in the cathedral or the vicinity at the critical time. You understand, sir?' Pride ended his opening words, delivered in a tone he had meant to exhibit relaxed confidence but which he felt had come out sounding more like a plea.

'Naturally,' answered the Dean. 'Meantime, any important developments?'

'Yes, sir. Post-mortem showed the victim died of asphyxia, not the head wound as we first believed. Also we've found his tea was laced. With sodium phenobarbitone.' He looked around the table slowly. 'The tea in his Thermos flask. He had it with him. Wasn't damaged by the fire.'

'Had he drunk any, Mr Pride?' This was Treasure.

Pride frowned. 'As a matter of fact he hadn't touched the tea, sir. The flask was full. There were no traces of drugs in the stomach.'

'Did he normally take sleeping pills in his tea, do you know?'

'Not according to his daughter,' Pride answered the banker again. 'And he never took pills of any kind. Didn't have any. Not that she knew of.'

'Was it . . . was it a dangerous quantity of phenobarb?' Treasure pressed while doing his best to make the question sound undramatic.

'No, sir. Enough to put him to sleep for a few hours, probably. Depends on whether he'd drunk one cup or two.'

'And you're saying somebody else put the drug in the tea?' questioned the Dean.

'Seems so, on the face of it, sir. They say he always had the flask with him when he arrived at four-thirty. Left it in the vergers' robing room during the service.'

'Where anyone would have access to it?' Treasure asked.

'Not anyone,' put in Ewart Jones carefully. 'Not anyone officiating at evensong, for instance. Or attending it. Not necessarily.'

'That's right,' said Algy merit. 'Suppose he'd leave it behind when he came to the clergy vestry before the service. To help the Dean robe.'

'But anyone not involved in the service could then get at the flask?' Treasure insisted. 'The vergers' room isn't locked when not in use?'

'Often not the room itself, which is next to the clergy vestry in the south choir aisle,' Bliter explained for the banker's benefit. 'Too many vergers going in and out all the time. They each have a locker there, though.'

'Mr Pounder used to leave his Thermos on the table. According to the head verger, sir,' said Pride. 'Didn't put it in his locker in case he didn't notice it after the service – and forgot to take it up to the library with him.'

'Except he forgot to drink the tea when he did get it there,' said Treasure.

'That's exactly what his daughter says, sir. Seems he'd become very forgetful lately. It's the most likely explanation.'

'And doesn't affect the circumstances of his death. Since he never drank the tea. Or the dope,' said Jones.

'I imagine the Chief Inspector would still like to know how the stuff got in the Thermos,' the banker commented.

'That's right, sir. And why.'

'More than a loose end.'

The policeman gave Treasure an appreciative nod. 'The tea could have been doctored before ever Pounder got to the cathedral,' said the Dean.

'We're taking that into account,' Pride replied. 'All the same, could I ask whether any of you gentlemen has any idea how the phenobarbitone was introduced?' He paused. There was no response. 'It's not something commonly prescribed these days. Would any of you have any in your possession or know of anyone else who has? Sodium phenobarbitone or phenobarbitone?'

'There's a difference between them?' asked Treasure.

'The sodium's a lot more soluble. Dissolves faster in liquid. The lab's fairly certain it was sodium in the flask.'

'I have some,' volunteered Algy Merit. 'Not sure which kind. Brand called Nembutal. Sovereign remedy for occasional sleeplessness. I didn't put any in Pounder's tea. And I doubt whether I had the opportunity.'

'I see, sir. Does anyone else have access to your supply?'

Merit shrugged. 'My sister, I suppose. But I'm quite sure she'd never touch it. You interviewed her last night,' which implied it was up to the Chief Inspector to do so again if he wasn't satisfied.

'Thank you, Canon Merit. Anyone else in possession of pheno-barbitone?'

Clive Brastow cleared his throat as if he was about to say something, then didn't.

'Will you all excuse me a moment?' Pride got up and went to the door where his detective constable had just appeared. The two conferred briefly. 'You don't mind if my colleague sits in?' said Pride returning to his seat: it was a rhetorical question and no one troubled to answer it. The younger man moved to a chair against the wall and produced a notebook.

The senior officer looked around the group slowly before continuing: 'I meant to mention we found the key to the Old Library. The one that went missing, Canon Jones. Not where you'd expect it. Lying on that grass square in the middle of Abbot's Cloister. Like it was thrown there.'

'Which indicates the murderer left by the cloister door, though the north door must still have been open,' observed Algy Merit unexpectedly.

'It could do, sir. Would you attach any significance to that?'

'Some, yes. Those of us who live north of the cathedral seldom use that door.'

'And it follows people who live in the cloisters always do, sir?'

'I didn't say that.'

'A common thief could have gone for either door,' suggested Bliter with spirit. He was the only cloister resident present.

'You're sure it was Pounder's key?' asked Treasure.

'We wondered that, sir. But now we're satisfied. Could I just ask Canon Jones, were you carrying a large leather document-case when you went to the cathedral at ten minutes past six last evening, sir?' The policeman's words had taken on a marginally more official ring.

'Yes. Didn't I tell you before?'

'No, you didn't, sir.'

'Well, it was to put the Magna Carta in. I had it inside my coat on both trips.'

'At six-twelve you were allegedly seen from inside the cathedral leaving the building with the case under your left arm, sir.'

'Prior to putting it back under my coat when I got outside, I expect.'

'Was there anything in it then, sir?'

'No, there wasn't.'

'Not the Magna Carta, sir?'

'Certainly not. Is this a game, Chief Inspector?'

'Are we allowed to know who saw the Canon?' the Dean interposed with unusual severity.

'The head verger, Mr Duggan, sir.'

'Does he say what he was doing in the cathedral at that time?' This was Merit.

'Seems he'd come back to fetch something he'd left in his locker, sir. A betting-shop receipt.'

'Is there anything else, Chief Inspector?' The Dean sounded tetchy.

'Afraid so, sir. We've identified the key because it carried Mr Pounder's fingerprints. Good clear ones.' Pride glanced briefly at the constable before he went on. 'And it's just been reported to me it also has two other prints on it. One we haven't identified as yet. The other belongs to Canon Jones.'

# Chapter Eleven

'Please sir, did they take your fingerprints, sir?' Jackson Minor trebled from the back row of desks.

'Did it hurt, sir?' sniggered Mead, the Third Form jester.

'Don't be daft, Mead,' chortled his neighbour, an angelic-looking child called Heyworth, while trying to elbow him in the groin under the desk.

'Have they arrested anyone, sir?' Mead persisted while retaliating with a tactical punch to Heyworth's right kidney. Heyworth had been leaning forward to protect his front against an expected assault.

'Swine!' shrieked the angelic one.

'Shut up, all of you. Mead, stop being a pain. Get on with your work,' commanded Minor Canon Twist from the master's desk on the podium in the painted brick classroom.

'But, sir . . .' Mead began a futile protest.

Few of the fourteen pupils, all choristers, took much notice of Twist's injunction. It wasn't that he couldn't keep order if he wanted, though he was no great disciplinarian. This morning his mind was on other things and his charges had sensed it.

This was the lower middle form at the choir school in East Street: the ten-year-olds. They were quite responsive to music theory but less to divinity: Twist taught both to the whole school and he was supposed to be teaching divinity now.

'Go on, sir. Tell us about the fingerprinting. Did you go to the police station?'

'No, I didn't.' He'd relented only to keep the record straight.

'You ink your fingers on a pad and press the tips on a card. Now, for heaven's sake . . .'

'Were you the only one, sir?'

'Are you under deep suspicion, sir?'

'Of course not. Mead, you're an ass.'

'Yes, sir,' the boy acknowledged proudly.

'Ee-oo! Ee-oo!' brayed the rest of the class in unison.

'So why did the fuzz take your dabs, sir?' asked Perkins when the noise died down. He was a sickly child, short-sighted, permanently excused games but grudgingly respected for alleged connections with the underworld; the others believed his father, a window cleaner by trade, was actually a successful burglar.

'I think they fingerprinted everyone who'd handled the Dean's mace or been in the Old Library yesterday.'

'Did they do Mrs Brastow, sir?'

'I don't know, Jackson. They may have done.'

'She was in the Old Library the day before. After matins.'

'Plenty of people were. Did you touch the mace, sir – the murder weapon?'

'Yes, as it happens. I'd taken it down from its bracket in the vestry. Yesterday, before evensong.' And Canon Jones had put it back, he remembered. They'd been examining the semi-precious stones in it, assessing its value. In the end they'd decided it didn't have much value. 'Now get on with your . . .'

'Please, sir, can Mead and I be your alibi, sir?'

'Certainly not, Heyworth.' But he was puzzled, and looked it. 'What alibi?' he enquired tentatively.

'We saw you in North Street, sir. Last night. At quarter to seven. Going into Miss Purse's flat, sir.'

'Ooo!' roared all the others, savouring the amatory implications of the disclosure and banging on their desks.

'Shut up, all of you,' ordered Twist, reddening. 'And, anyway, it was earlier when I went . . . there.' More 'ooing' followed.

'It was quarter to by Mead's watch, sir. It's a new one. Show him your watch, Mead.'

Mead jumped to his feet, pulled back his sleeve and showed

the whole form, twirling his upraised fist. 'It was a quarter to, sir,' he corroborated. 'We'd been to Heyworth's house to get his conjuring set. It was when we'd been going there we saw Miss Purse going home.'

'That was twenty to. Five minutes before we saw you, sir.'

'We can alibi both of you, sir.'

'Well, we don't need alibis, thank you.' And a fat lot of good an alibi for quarter to seven would be. 'Now get on with your essays. Right now. Or else.' They did, because this time the class consensus was that he probably meant it.

Twist affected to be marking the papers he had in front of him but his mind was elsewhere. He knew the boys were right. He'd told her he hadn't got to her place till later than she said, but she'd insisted they'd been together much earlier. She'd been concerned that she could witness where he'd been in the half-hour that mattered. But if she hadn't got home till six-forty herself, how could they have been together before then?

Only briefly did he wonder how she'd come to be so wrong. He didn't wonder at all where she'd been herself at the time she'd insisted she could vouch for him, and – it followed – when he should have been able to vouch for her. But, then, Gerard Twist tended to think mostly of himself.

'It was the lawyer who said it had to be that way. Young fellow. Said him and the bank manager would need to be there.' Harry Jakes, who had just come in, hung his overcoat on the back of the kitchen door.

'So we could look at our own property? I think that's a liberty,' Nora Jakes commented breathily from the cooker where she was preparing the midday meal.

'Not our property. Not till after we've got a death certificate, they said.' He pulled out a chair from the table and sat down.

'But Dad made you his executor. I remember.'

'Didn't make any difference. Not for today.'

'So you went to the bank? You and the lawyer?'

'That's right. And we saw the manager. In his office. And he sent for the cash-box your dad kept there. That's after the lawyer said who I was. Showed the will.'

'Lot of red tape, seems to me.'

'Got to be. For the death duties. Got to prove to the tax people everything's above board.'

'What death duties? Dad didn't leave enough for that.' She looked around again at her husband. 'He didn't, did he?'

'There was a little account-book in the box. A lot of cash. And pass-books with two building societies,' he detailed carefully. 'Cash had to be counted. Then put back. Till after we get probate.'

'How much cash was there?'

'Better sit down.' He knew shocks were bad for her – for her heart: the doctor had said so after that last turn.

'More than you expected, was it?' She left what she was doing and sat at the table, wiping her hands on the pinafore she had on.

He took a piece of paper from his pocket. 'Thirteen thousand, four hundred pounds. That's the cash. All in twenty-pound notes. In the box.' He paused, watching her reaction before going on. 'He'd put another eighteen thousand in the building societies. He never told you?'

Her mouth had opened in astonishment. She shook her head slowly in denial. For a few moments she said nothing, then she offered weakly: 'Where did Dad get all that?'

'That's what the bank manager was asking. Tactful like, but that's what he meant. You sure your dad never mentioned . . . ?'

'Course I'm sure. Oh dear. It's made me feel all funny.'

'You going to be all right, love?'

'I think so.' She took several deep breaths. 'How long had he had it?'

'Seems like since he put the box in the bank. That's three years ago this month. So the manager said. He had records. And it fits with when Dad started the entries in the account-book. Very neat they are. Meticulous.'

'That's Dad all over.'

'Seems he went to the box regular. Twice in a day at the end of every month.'

'To take money out?'

He nodded. 'And the pass-books. He took money to put in the building societies. They both got branches in Market Square. Then he must have taken the pass-books again.'

'How much did you say in the building societies?'

'Nine thousand each. Plus interest over the three years. His account-book shows he took six hundred a month from the box. He . . . he put five hundred in the societies. Two-fifty in each. Don't know what he did with the other hundred. But it was six hundred altogether every month. Like clockwork, it seems.'

'He didn't need the hundred for spending. He had his pension for that.'

Jakes shrugged. 'Fact is, according to that account-book, he started with thirty-five thousand in cash. What's left is all in brand-new notes. Hundreds of 'em. With consecutive numbers. In packs of a thousand pounds. Like they all came in one lot.'

'They weren't stolen? Oh Lord, say they weren't stolen.'

'They weren't. Or else it's never been reported. The bank manger checked. The lawyer asked him.'

'That was a nerve.' Her jaw had tightened.

'No, it was best to check, I said. So far as they could. The manager got the dates the notes were issued. Approximate anyway. From the Bank of England. Seems they're four years old. Doesn't mean he got the money four years ago.'

'But why did he get it? And why put it in a box in the bank?'

'Most likely he was laundering it, love.'

'I don't understand.'

'Making it look respectable. More respectable,' he added quickly after watching her frightened reaction. 'How ever he got the money, seems he didn't want people to know. Not even us. So he was paying it into building societies. Gradual. To look like it was savings. Earnings.'

'Earnings? How could my dad have . . . ?'

'From tips he could have been getting. For showing tourists round the cathedral.'

'But he'd never have got that much. Not every month.'

'Except it was more believable that way than if he'd got a lump sum. One he couldn't explain. Like thirty-five thousand. It's not as if he did the pools. And he didn't have any premium bonds that we know of. Anyway, winnings could be explained.'

'I suppose so. But not telling us. When he knew we'd find out some day.'

'What's the betting he'd have told us? In two years or so. When all the money would have been in savings accounts. It was just . . .'

'That he died. Too soon. Oh dear.' She wiped her eyes. The look of apprehension deepened. 'So will we have to explain anything?'

'Maybe, the lawyer said. But we're to leave it to him. Not to say anything to anyone. Bank manager agreed.' He paused. 'There's something else. In the will. Your dad added to it. A year ago. He left five thousand pounds to someone. To Cindy Larks.'

'That girl in the choir?'

'That's right. It's to pay for voice training for her. That's what it says. Very thoughtful, the bank manager said. Everything else is left to you.'

'Typical of Dad. Helping deserving people. Those in need.'


'You sure I'm not stopping anything? Dropping in like this? Not interrupting the Muse?'

Jennifer Bliter's affected accent and high, piercing voice could have stopped a lot of things, and interrupted a brass quartet if she put her mind to it – was Margaret Hitt's unvoiced opinion. Aloud she said: 'Not at all. I always have a coffee break at eleven.' She put the tray on the table beside her typewriter. 'Milk and sugar? Help yourself.'

The two women were in Mrs Hitt's small workroom beside the kitchen at the back of the Deanery. It was the place where she did her ironing and wrote her novels. The furnishings and general clutter reflected the room's dual function. The table was before a window that looked over a pretty corner of the garden.

'I only came to bring back the book really.' The last word

spoiled the validity of the claim – as did the speaker's state of only mildly suppressed excitement. 'One of my rules. Never hang on to a borrowed book. Take it back straight away. As soon as you've read it. Earns you the privilege of borrowing another. Lord Cunningham taught me that. Admiral of the Fleet, Lord Cunningham. When I was a very young girl. Dear man. Close friend of Daddy's.' She opened her bag. 'No, I won't smoke.' She put back the cigarette-packet.

'Feel free to take another book.' The Dean's wife waved at the painted, over-full shelves that occupied most of two walls.

'More biography, then.' Mrs Bliter took down a volume, then sat abruptly, leafing through it but not to any evident purpose. 'Such a drag my book-buying days are over. The cost is quite prohibitive now. Different for writers, I expect. When books are tax deductible.'

'Not very different. And only reference books. I suppose one buys more as a result.'

Mrs Bliter closed the volume sharply. 'I should take up writing again. I used to write, you know? Nothing published. I couldn't be bothered at the time. Now it'd be different. With you to guide and advise. It's what I needed before. The company of other writers.'

'I'd be glad to look at anything for you.'

'Thank you, Margaret.' They had not long been on Christian-name terms: Mrs Bliter consciously renewed the licence at each meeting. 'There's drama all about us, of course. Right here, in Litchester.'

'Has been today, certainly.'

'Every day. For those with the imagination to spot it. Trollope showed us how.'

'You enjoy him?' came the distinct overtone that the speaker didn't.

'His pictures of cathedral life. The close. The community. The politics.'

'Wonder how he'd have coped with the murder of Mr Pounder?

If he'd allowed it to happen in Barchester? Life's sterner than Trollope at the moment.'

'He had villains. And chapter quarrels. And wives exchanging views. In confidence' – Mrs Bliter took a sip of her coffee – 'do you trust Donald Welt?'

Mrs Hitt was satisfied she now knew the reason for the call. 'He's a very fine musician.'

'I meant his morals. D'you think he has standards? Subscribes to any code of decency?'

'I hardly know him that well.'

'You know he's an atheist?'

'Agnostic, I thought. So many of us are for periods in our lives. He makes no bones about it.'

'He's also divorced.'

The other woman shrugged. 'That's not secret, either. An unfortunate marriage, I gather. My husband and the rest of the Chapter knew about it before he was appointed here. It's not as though he's in holy orders, after all.'

'Not from a very good background, either. Grammar school, I understand,' observed the admiral's daughter stiffly. 'Young women find him attractive. Small rugged men often have that effect.'

The Dean's wife wondered whether Jennifer Bliter also found the organist attractive. She was hardly young but her comments so far could have been inspired by jealousy. 'I suppose he's entitled to a love life.'

'You think he should be allowed to seduce the girls in the choir?'

'In principle, no. In practice, it depends on which girls. Two or three of them are young women. Eighteen-year-olds.' She paused. 'You meant the older girls?'

'Yes. But it still seems wrong.'

'You have proof?'

'That he has one of them come to his house regularly. At night.'

'Cindy Larks. He gives her singing lessons, I believe. Because she works in the daytime.'

'Anyone in a position of authority who takes personal advantage of that position . . .' Mrs Bliter snorted but didn't go on with the sentence. Instead she said: 'So perhaps that part's not important. My husband thinks it isn't. Of course, Percy is careful about criticism. He's full of Christian charity.' She didn't add that Percy was also very aware of his lowly status in the cathedral hierarchy: it accounted for his sense of vulnerability and the pains he took not to make enemies.

'You said that part's not important. There's another?'

'That I should have reported to the police. I haven't. It's . . . difficult.'

'Can I be of help? It is something Percy knows about?'

'Not yet. We had two policemen round this morning. Percy left for the Chapter House straight after.' She paused. 'Then the police went next door. To Donald Welt's. He didn't ask them in. They had to interview him on the doorstep. I overheard every word. Couldn't help it.'

'Presumably he had nothing he minded others knowing.'

Mrs Bliter arched her over-plucked eyebrows. 'Just before half past six last night Dr Welt went into the cathedral. By the cloister door. And doing his best not to be seen.'

'But you saw him?'

'By chance, yes. Later he denied it. Not directly to me.'

'To the police?'

'As good as. He told them he left the cathedral after evensong. At a quarter to six.'

'Did he admit to being out at all later?'

'Yes. For three-quarters of an hour from half-six. For dinner in the town. But he said he hadn't been into the cathedral. I couldn't believe it.'

'And you think he might have been involved in Mr Pounder's death?'

Jennifer Bliter swallowed at the directness of the question. 'I don't say that. But why deny being in the cathedral at a critical time? He was known to be rabidly in favour of selling the Magna Carta,' she added pointedly.

'Is that so? To fund the musical establishment, I expect. Of itself that doesn't mean . . .'

'I believe Pounder was a strict moralist. If he'd found out about Welt's philandering with the girl choristers . . .' Again she stopped in mid-sentence, aware she had gone too far – much too far, judging from the look on the face of her hostess. 'D'you think it's my duty to tell the police?'

'Might it not be better to tell Donald Welt – that you saw him go into the cathedral?'

'What if he reacted violently? He has a dreadful temper. I've always thought he could be dangerous.'

The wretched woman possibly had a point there. 'Would you like me to discuss it with my husband? To have him speak to Dr Welt?'

'Very much so. If it's not making trouble for him?' Margaret Hitt had already decided where the potential trouble lay.

# Chapter Twelve

'They haven't arrested your father. Or anything like it.'

'Going to the police station for questioning doesn't seem far off,' Glynis Jones answered Treasure uncertainly as they walked across the top of Bridge Street and into Market Square.

It was twelve-thirty. The girl had kept the arrangement to call for the banker at his hotel after getting back from her morning's work. They were going to a pub for lunch. The rain had stopped. The sun was shining fitfully, but it had grown colder.

'He's free to leave any time he chooses. But it makes a lot of sense to clear things up with the police straight away,' Treasure offered with more confidence than he felt. 'He's got his lawyer with him.'

'Only because you insisted.'

'Your father wasn't crazy about the idea. Just another sensible precaution, I thought.'

He steered her along the south side of the crowded, ancient square. It was now a paved pedestrian precinct with trees in concrete tubs, benches, and a boarded-up street café closed for the winter but festooned – like the tree – with coloured lights and tinsel decorations supplied by the municipality to mark the Yuletide. There was a group of open market stalls in the centre, the Christmas merchandise displayed making a brave, colourful contrast under the sombre wet roof coverings.

The buildings surrounding the square were mostly of Tudor and Georgian origin rendered in white or the shade of pink approved by the vigilant Litchester Preservation Group. The shops at ground level carried cheerful adornments involving imitation snow appropriate to the festive season if not entirely to the weather forecast which predicted fog and rain.

'Good thing Mummy's away for the day. A Mothers' Union binge somewhere. You sure I shouldn't be waiting at the police station?'

'Positive. Wouldn't achieve anything – except bug your father and possibly start rumours. Where did you say this Daras family farm was?' He had promised her father he would keep her occupied.

'Much Stratton. Small village nine miles from here.'

'On the way to?'

'Nowhere in particular.'

'And you'd never heard of this Daras before?'

'Not till you asked me to enquire. His name's Joshua. Some people know him. Two of the farmers I've seen this morning. But he doesn't fraternise. Got a reputation as a weirdo. Applies to the whole family. Don't farm much, either. About fifty acres, and that's mostly gone to scrub and rough pasture.'

'And is pretty small by any standards?'

'Sure. Seems they used to be important landowners, though. They still own farms leased to other people. You didn't say why you wanted to know about them.'

'Tell you in a minute.' He took her arm, motioning her to stop. 'The man in the bowler coming out of the pub. Remember him?'

'Yes. Last night at the station. He got off your train. In a hurry then as well. But not so furtive.'

'That's what I thought.' They watched Len Hawker turn a corner out of the square. 'What's round there?'

'Public loos and the bus terminus.'

'D'you mind following him?'

She smirked. 'So long as he's catching a bus.'

The short, bending lane they entered disgorged onto an open area where a dozen or so mostly double-decker red buses were docked or else manoeuvring alongside raised passenger-islands. Overlooking this scene, at their immediate right, was an unprepossessing Victorian building fronted at ground-floor level by a wide, open-sided shelter with a green glass roof and wrought-iron supports.

The two were just in time to see their quarry leave the shelter and dodge in front of a moving bus. They also saw the other male figure who had entered the lane just ahead of them quickly follow him when the bus had passed.

They watched Hawker cross almost the width of the terminus, then consult the conversing driver and conductor of a stationary and quite elderly double-decker, painted yellow and black. Its destination board announced 'The Strattons'. It was parked at the furthest distance from the terminal building with a group of three others – all with differing and somehow unauthoritative kinds of livery.

'Country bus. Independent operator,' Glynis announced, unprompted. 'Goes four times a day to the Strattons.'

'And Much Stratton's . . . ?'

'One of those Strattons, yes. There's Much, Middle and Stratton Parva.' She looked at him quizzically. 'Is this a coincidence? I mean with Daras living there.'

'Not entirely.'

'Well, if you're interested, the bus leaves at quarter to. In six minutes. And it looks as if Rory Duggan's going, too.' Like Treasure and the girl, the man, she'd just identified had hung back while Hawker had been making enquiries. Now they watched him get on the bus after Hawker. He chose the lower deck after watching the other man climb to the upper. The bus was already half-full.

'Who's Rory Duggan?'

'The head verger's awful youngest son. Dropout. His father's not much better, if you ask me. Who's the fellow he's following?'

He told her – as much as he knew, adding: 'Could you get your car here in six minutes?'

'Yes, if you're that interested in Mr Hawker's movements. You want to follow the bus?'

'I want to know if he's going to see Daras.'

'If he does, it'll be more of a coincidence?'

'That, and very revealing.'

Twenty minutes later the two were sitting in the Suzuki, which was parked in a side-road opposite the bus stop in the centre of Much Stratton. They had both decided that tailing the bus through country lanes was too conspicuous, so they had driven on ahead, risking that Hawker might get off earlier than they expected.

The dog Jingles was in the car, perched alert if uncomfortable between the two front seats. She had been asleep in the car when Glynis had fetched it.

'Another sandwich?' Glynis offered.

They had also had time to pick up food.

'Yes, please. And here's the bus.' He pointed to the disembodied yellow top advancing in the middle distance along bare cropped hedgerows, and now just beyond the village outskirts. 'You reckon he'll get off at the stop after this one?'

'If he knows exactly where the Daras farm is. And assuming he's going to it.' She started the engine.

'Well, at least he's still aboard. So's Duggan,' said Treasure. Neither of the men were amongst the half-dozen passengers who got off, but the conductor had gone up to the top deck and spoken to Hawker, who could be seen nodding in thanks for something. 'Hawker's being told he wants the next stop,' the banker added. 'So let's go.'

Glynis deftly raced the Suzuki ahead. Two minutes later, when the bus stopped again, just beyond a country crossroads and beside a call-box, she had the car pulled into a gate-opening two hundred yards behind.

'Is that Hawker getting off now?' Treasure's view was partly obstructed by the hedge.

'And Duggan. Oh, that was clever. Slipped off behind Hawker's back while Hawker was talking to the conductor. Now he's belting along this way as if he had some reason.'

'Hope he hasn't. Does he know you?'

'He might do. Anyway, he's gone into hiding on our left.'

After a glance behind to see what Hawker was doing, the young Irishman had ducked down the narrow side road.

Hawker had meantime walked a little further in the direction the bus had taken. Then he stopped, looked dubiously both ways along the quite empty road before crossing to the farm gate opposite. He tried the gate which wouldn't budge. Slowly and very gingerly he climbed over, straightened his hat and overcoat on the other side, then set off along whatever path lay beyond and whose nature was obscured from the watchers in the car, except they could see it was tree-lined.

A moment later Duggan reappeared in the main road, crossed in a hurry, scampered along below the cover of the hedge and, after a brief observation, vaulted the gate.

'Nice to have intentions so clearly defined,' observed Treasure. 'That's definitely the Daras farm gate?'

'According to my directions.'

'Then, shall we join the others?'

'Better give them a decent start.'

They left the car where it was, the girl pausing to lock it, while Treasure set off briskly along the road. 'Now we've established what they're up to, I'm quite anxious to meet Mr Joshua Daras,' he said. 'Especially in the company of Hawker. I'd guess your Irish friend is just inquisitive.'

'Inquisitive and on the make if he's running to form,' the girl replied, hurrying to catch up, with Jingles trotting behind her. 'That's not friendly,' she said when they had crossed the road to the gate. She was pointing to the barbed wire laid along the top bar. 'No wonder Hawker was careful. Padlocked, too.'

There was also a painted notice nailed to the gate and bearing the legend 'Private Property. Trespassers Prosecuted.'

The farm track they followed when they had safely surmounted the first obstacle was deep in undisturbed beech and horsechestnut leaves. In places it was rutted and waterlogged, but the ruts looked old and not the result of use during the recent rains. The overgrown track progressed in a wide curve, the view on either side obscured by the height of the untamed brambles and scrub that in some places spewed out underfoot.

'Shouldn't think they go out much,' said Treasure.

'And they certainly don't encourage callers,' remarked the girl. It was as she spoke that the unmistakable sound of a shot rang out, and not far away. It was followed by a short burst of ferocious barking, then the pained shriek of a sharply disciplined dog and the thump of running footsteps coming towards them.

'Quick.' Treasure pulled her off the path, through the undergrowth and behind a huge tree-trunk. The scrub fell back again behind them. Jingles had come, too, with no prompting.

Rory Duggan doubled past. His face was ashen, and his expression terrified. He looked over his shoulder, evidently fearing pursuit. Now he turned about, moving backwards on his toes, and listening. It seemed there was no one behind him, but when he resumed normal running he had hardly reduced the pace.

'Want to go back?' asked Treasure as the Irishman disappeared.

'Not on your life. Not with you and Jingles for protection,' she insisted, the bravado a bit forced. They waited a few moments before moving off again.

A hundred yards onwards the path broadened abruptly into a yard set with broken cobbles and decorated by a single stalking, inquisitive cockerel. On the far side was a dilapidated farmhouse, and Treasure was almost sure he saw the front door shut as it came into view. An Alsatian dog was chained to a kennel near the door. The dog whimpered while watching the newcomers. Jingles watched the dog.

Close by, on the right, were some empty pigsties. Beyond these stood a row of three lurching outhouses, each component seeming to rely on the next for support and to prevent imminent collapse. The centre structure was a barn – two storeys with a gable and loft hoist at the front. It was open-ended at ground level, though whether by design and not deterioration it was difficult to determine. It was also full of ewe sheep.

One of the sheep was perched on a foot-high plinth at the front looking as conspicuous as the 'car of the week' in a showroom window. Seated behind the ewe was an old woman in a fur coat. She had a woollen scarf wrapped round her head and a black patch over one eye. She was milking the sheep into a metal receptacle let into the plinth: the top was just discernible under the animal's rear quarters.

'Good afternoon. My name is Treasure.'

There was no verbal response, only a suspicious one-eyed assessment from both the human addressed and the ewe – the latter's concern being evidently over Jingles. The little dog had settled in front of the plinth, head on one side, watching the milking process with every appearance of canine incredulity.

'Dorset Horns, are they?' asked Glynis brightly, nodding at the dozen or so anxious sheep assembled but not penned in the building behind.

'Quite right, Missy,' replied the woman in a coarse accent.

'They're the autumn lambers. I expect you keep . . .'

'Freislands for summer milk. Nothing like 'em.' The speaker smacked the ewe on the rump. It skipped off the plinth and another immediately took its place.

'Expect you make . . .'

'Cheese and yoghurt. Is that what you've come for? Only enough for our own needs. And special friends.' The tone made it clear the two visitors didn't qualify. 'You know you be trespassing?' But the sharp glance at the end was not unkindly.

'Actually, we've come to see your brother, Miss Daras . . .'

'Have you now, Missy? Make an appointment, did you? He's a very busy man. So he says.' The last remark seemed to fill the speaker with uncontrollable mirth. For a few moments she rocked to and fro on her chair, revealing in the process that it was very probably by Sheraton – just as the coat she had on was undoubtedly mink, if rather old mink. Eventually Miss Daras pulled herself together and went back to milking the sheep.

'I did try to reach you by telephone,' offered Treasure.

If her own previous comment had tickled the old woman, this one induced an actually frightening paroxysm of hilarity.

'Telephone,' she cackled, wiping her visible eye and again baring her few remaining front teeth. 'Telephone. Oh, that's a good one.'

'You mean you're still pre-electric,' smiled Glynis.

This time Miss Daras was so consumed with laughter she slid off her chair at the front on to her knees and had to be helped back by the questioner. 'Pre-electric. Pre-electric,' she gargled hoarsely. 'Lord help you, we haven't got the gas yet.'

'Well, I think we should call on Mr Daras. Good to have met you . . .'

'You can try,' the old crone interrupted Treasure. 'Front door's over there. Mind the dog.'

'We heard a shot earlier.'

'Did you now, Missy? Got to protect ourselves. Protect our virtue.' But, instead of pealing with laughter at what the others took to be a witticism, the speaker was re-applying herself assiduously to her main task.

There was no knocker, though there was a space denoting where one had been long ago. The callers – particularly Jingles – had been careful to line themselves on the side of the door furthest from the Alsatian. The dog barked at them unceasingly and with increasing fervour the closer they came, straining and pulling on it chain, wrestling to break free, sometimes rolling about in contortions, sometimes towering on its hind legs. All this induced thoroughly worried noises from Jingles and mute but matching concern from both her companions.

Treasure rapped sharply on the peeled, greyed paintwork of the door, which was opened immediately by a scrawny, middle-aged woman smoking a clay pipe. Behind her was a sniggering girl of about twenty with a young baby in her arms. The older female had on a man's cap and an aged overcoat open over a dirty cotton dress. There were carpet slippers on her thick-stockinged feet. The girl, big and buxom, wore blue overalls and her hair in dirty ringlets.

'We've called to see Mr Daras,' announced Treasure firmly. 'Sorry to have disturbed your dog.'

'Right. This way, then,' said the girl in a broad country burr and an implication that they might have been expected. She scuffed her bare feet through the thick layer of straw covering the flagstone floor as she conducted them across the square, empty hall. ''Ee's in the dining,' she added, throwing open a door.

Both visitors caught their breath.

The big room was over-furnished – like an antique showroom with nothing displayed to advantage.

In the middle was a long, thick medieval oak table with its centre opposite the door on one side and a huge fireplace on the other. Logs were burning briskly in the hearth. Most of the chairs around the table matched the one Miss Daras had been using outside. The floor was covered in Oriental rugs of different sizes and thickly overlapping.

At one end of the room was a *chaise longue,* a number of richly upholstered chairs and occasional tables all wedged in front of a formidable and intricately carved Welsh dresser. The other end was dominated by a massive double bed, unmade and partly inhabited. This was hemmed in by more chairs, cabinets, and a glazed bookcase crammed with china and glass.

It seemed every available section of wall space was taken up with oil paintings. Every flat surface was covered with bric-à-brac, with silver boxes, vases, bowls, and candlesticks and candelabra – all except the centre of the table where there was evidence a meal was in progress.

The remains of two cold chickens and a ham were displayed on a silver serving plate balanced on a small and presumably battery-operated television receiver. Silver vegetable-dishes, a soup-tureen, a scattering of apples and pears and a cheeseboard were grouped around. Some empty beer-cans lay upturned beside a much less plebeian silver tankard.

In the bed a girl was laying on her stomach with her face peering over the bottom board. She was not unlike the young woman with the baby, but younger – about sixteen. She was clad in a short cotton shift. Her concentration and both her arms were sternly engaged.

Behind the food sat a very old man. He was small and shrivelled.

There was little hair on the tight skin of his wide domed head but plenty protruding from the orifices of ears and nose, and in uneven wisps from behind his jawbone. The parched skin of his face was patched with red blobs, most noticeably below the eyes – dark sunken eyes that searched and strained over the top of the gold half-spectacles perched on the end of a surprisingly bulbous nose. He was clothed in army uniform – khaki battle dress tunic and trousers that were comically over-sized. Under the tunic collar the tops of striped flannel pyjamas protruded; under the table running shoes encased feet protruding below sockless white bony legs.

'Stand still and be recognised. Move and 'ee's dead. Hold it on 'im, girl. Hold it!' cried the old man in a frenzy of ascending yokelry, the pitch so high at the suddenly attenuated finish it seemed he might have strained something. Although an accusing mittened finger remained pointing at the end of a wavering, out-stretched arm, behind it the head slumped to nearly table level.

'They're all mad. Help me,' pleaded Len Hawker, who had dared to look round from where he was kneeling, bowler hat askew, well inside the room. The shot-gun the girl was levelling was pointing directly at his chest.

# Chapter Thirteen

'Mr Daras?' questioned the banker formally. 'My name's Treasure. This is Miss Jones.' There was an ominous click behind him. He didn't want to look over his shoulder but sensed that he and Glynis had just been locked inside the room by the two women who had ushered them in and who were now flanking them. 'I can't imagine what Mr Hawker here . . .'

'Raping an' ravaging in my domain, is it? Sorry you'll be in the latter day. Won't they, sisters?'

'Aah!' exclaimed the three women in a sort of unison but with varying degrees of keenness. The girl on the bed was the most enthusiastic.

'Sorry this man be already. Dispoiling our sister Ethel in the midst of her work. Her milking.' Daras seemed to have recovered his strength but his voice was operating in a lower register than before and with less vigour.

'Whatever Mr Hawker was doing, I'm quite sure he wasn't assaulting the lady milking the sheep,' replied Treasure firmly. 'Please tell that young lady to put the gun down. Now.'

'You'll not be a rapist as well – not bringing a young nubile wench along with you?' The old man's beady gaze swept Glynis lasciviously from head to toe and back again before reverting to regard the quaking Hawker. "Ee be a rapist, though. Going in custody he is. A prey on sisters, daughters and grand-daughters.'

'And great grand-daughters,' cried the girl on the bed.

'Mr Hawker here is a private investigator,' said Glynis coolly, advancing to stand beside that unfortunate. 'He's a sort of police-man. I think you'd better put the gun away, don't you? Otherwise the whole lot of you will be going into custody. And not just for threats with a loaded shotgun. From great grand-daughters. Marvellous family likeness, Mr Daras. Are your sons-in-law about?'

'Put it down, Nabar,' ordered Daras slowly after a pause for contemplation. 'It's not loaded, Missy. Show her it's not loaded.'

The girl Nabar sniggered, bounced up on the bed, and broke open the gun. With exaggerated movements she exposed to everybody present not only the empty breach but also a calculatedly generous amount of bare bosom.

Hawker staggered awkwardly to his feet, removed his bowler, and wiped his brow with his chequered handkerchief. 'The other one was loaded,' he cried in outrage. 'The one they fired outside. When they set the dog on me. I'm very upset. Please make him let me go.'

'Trespassing you were then. Trespassing you are now. Man can't be too careful,' Daras went on hurriedly and addressing himself to Treasure. 'Not living out here he can't. Need to put the fear of Almighty God in prowlers.' He lifted his arms heavenwards. 'An' beseech His protection for deserving womenfolk.'

'Amen,' chanted the three Daras women.

The old man's arms came down. 'Nothing for investigations, though. Nothing . . . nothing unnatural here.' Now the look he switched to Glynis was full of calculation. 'And people are welcome who come in peace. Like some tea?'

'We'd like you to let Mr Hawker go, with safe conduct off your property,' said Treasure.

The old man nodded malevolently at his early captive. 'Bugger off, and don't 'ee ever come back,' he admonished.

Hawker hesitated, but on an indication from Treasure he turned about and shuffled out through the door that the older women had unlocked and was holding open for him. He was limping awkwardly. The woman left, too, followed by the girl with the baby.

'And now we'd be grateful for some information, Mr Daras,' continued Treasure, sensing that the ascendancy established by

Glynis was still applying. 'I believe you're acquainted with Mr Pounder, the Dean's verger in Litchester.'

'Go and put some clothes on, Nabar,' was Daras's first response.

Nabar slid off the bed, in the process managing to reveal several sections of bare anatomy that hadn't been exhibited already. She left the gun lying on the covers and slunk across the room preening her auburn hair and slowly pulling up a strap of her slip. Her eyes were on Treasure most of the time and she purposely brushed her thigh against his as she passed on her way out of the room. She paused at the door to turn, make a face, and poke her tongue out at Glynis.

'Darlin' sweet child,' said Daras when the door closed behind the girl. 'Wouldn't hurt a fly. Warm enough for you 'ere, is it? Live mostly in 'ere we do. Saves fuel. Terrible poor we are today.' He narrowed his gaze. 'Neville Pounder sent you, then.'

The banker nodded, because figuratively the assumption was true. It appeared his hunch had paid off. 'To talk about the Magna Carta.'

'That's over. Long since.' Now there was suspicion on the crinkled face. One hand went to stroking the huge nose. 'Neville didn't come hisself?'

'No.' It seemed certain also that the news of Neville's awful demise had not come either.

'Couldn't come here again hisself. Wouldn't have it. Not pleading for 'er. Not the daughter taken in adultery. Not Beryl. Not the flesh of my flesh gone second-hand to a fornicator. Dead he is. Dead he ought to be as well. And her and her bitch child could be dead with him. That's for all I mind.' Daras retched and spat over his shoulder into the fire. He turned back to the two with a look of blatant malevolence.

'You and Mr Pounder were in the Army together?' put in Glynis, who, studiously unruffled, had seated herself at the table. Jingles, less relaxed, jumped into her lap.

'He told you that? And good friends one time. Best he got of the friendship, too.'

'He told us about the Magna Carta,' said Glynis, figuring it was time for another try in that area. 'More fool him.'

'The copy,' Treasure offered.

'Oh ay? Which copy would that be.' The eyes narrowed into slits.

'The Daras family copy,' confirmed the banker blandly and, judging from the other's interested reaction, confident he had taken the right direction.

'Lost that was. Long since. Terrible shame.'

'Came down through the family, I suppose? From the time of the scriptorium?'

The old man looked about him as if to enjoin the attention of others and not just his two hearers. 'County Sheriff he were. King's representative. My ancestor.'

'Powerful gentry,' offered Glynis quite softly. 'What happened, I wonder?'

'Come to this,' Daras replied in a whisper, his gaze now dolefully contemplating the cluttered board before him and seeming metaphorically to be reflecting on the present sad state of his family affairs. But it was the lion's contraction before the leap. Without warning he jumped to his feet, his arms scattering food and utensils. 'What happened?' he cried. 'Swindled we've been on every hand. Snared by usurers. In league with Beryl and 'er whorey daughter. That's who sent you. Tell us the truth, then!' He thumped his fists down on the table and left them there, while the rest of him subsided back into the chair, his chest heaving, his whole countenance a dangerous shade of purple.

'Nobody sent us, Mr Daras,' said Treasure. 'Not even poor Mr Pounder, I'm afraid. Not directly. We came because we're interested in Magna Carta copies. We thought you might have one. For sale.' Then he included as an afterthought 'Ready money, of course.'

Daras looked about him as though checking his whereabouts. The rancour had evaporated and the face resumed its blotchy norm. 'Very hard to come by.' He flashed a conspiratorial glance at both his hearers in turn. 'Good ones are. Very hard.'

'Are they as good as the original?'

'Can't tell the difference, most folk can't. Haven't got the knowledge.'

'Could you show us one?' asked Glynis.

Daras diminished further in his seat. 'Show you one, Missy? Now, how could I show you something as I haven't got?' he offered guardedly, then turned to Treasure. 'Supposing I knew someone? Let's say someone knowing where there's a copy. One that'd pass as genuine, like . . . like.' He stopped at this, rubbed his chest, then took several deep breaths before continuing. 'How much? How much of this ready money you got on offer?'

'Mr Treasure is an important banker,' Glynis volunteered across the table.

Daras's searching gaze remained on Treasure.

'As much as would be needed, Mr Daras. Perhaps five thousand pounds.'

Daras convulsed with laughter was not an edifying sight: so many of his teeth were missing. The mirth was eventually subdued by a fit of coughing. He wiped his eyes and mouth with a revoltingly dirty handkerchief. '"Perhaps five thousand pounds,"' he mimicked. 'That wouldn't buy the seal.'

'So how much more money would buy a copy? One as good as any you've sold already? The one you sold to Pounder? How much did that fetch?'

Treasure knew he'd made a mistake the moment the words were issued. Pumping Daras had been like playing a hooked fish, but this time the banker had reeled in when he should still have been letting the catch run free.

'Out of my house! Be gone! Out of my house!' the old man cried. He stumbled across to the bed, clutched the shotgun and began searching through the pockets of his tunic. At the same time the doors had burst open and the three women reappeared.

'Are they hurting you, Grandpa?' called the one with the baby.

'Can I lay into 'er, Grandpa? Tear her things?' pleaded the still scantily clothed Nabar with relish, and moving forward eagerly, pushed on by the older woman from behind.

Glynis jumped up and swung her chair around. Jingles, peremptorily unseated, began barking fiercely at her feet. Treasure had already moved up beside them. 'Calm down, all of you,' he ordered distinctly. 'We're leaving now, Mr Daras. If either of us is hurt by anybody or any animal, I'll see it costs you this house. This house, you understand, and all the things in it. Plus every penny you possess. Is that clear?'

'Get out,' Daras repeated, but with less venom and hardly any power. He hadn't succeeded in finding cartridges for the gun, which he was still cradling with the breach open. 'Beryl sent 'un. That's for sure,' he advised the three women. 'Spies they are. Spies.' He fell back into his chair as the women stood aside to make a gangway.

'Your threat about this place made him go quite white,' said Glynis as she and Treasure left the farmyard and entered the lane to the main road.

They had emerged unscathed. Even the chained Alsatian had regarded them with indifference. Ethel and the sheep were nowhere to be seen. Jingles, who had been trotting ahead, now watched them pass as, with an urgent look in her eyes, she watered the base of the first large tree along the path.

'One cares most about holding on to territorial boundaries,' said the banker glancing at the animal but meaning Daras.

'Especially when in reduced circumstances. I told you, he still leases out several farms in the area. Can't produce much. This one, what's left of it, used to be the home farm.'

'No stately family home as well?'

'There used to be. Fell down in the last century. Neighbours say Joshua Daras cut the family off from the rest of the community more than forty years ago. When his wife died.'

'Know what she died of?'

'Officially natural causes. But the word is she never got over the effects of being raped. By an Italian prisoner of war who'd been working on the farm. That's what one of my clients told me this morning.'

'You didn't mention it earlier.'

'Frankly, I didn't believe it earlier. Do now. There's a lot of scandal in village talk. You never know the truth for certain.'

'So his fixation with rape has a reason in fact?'

'Excuse more like,' said the girl slowly. 'All that business of protecting virtue is most likely a front for something nastier. Much nastier.'

'I don't follow.'

'That's because you're not exposed to isolated country communities. Isolation for some of the families becomes a way of life. They fall into being self-sufficient. In every way.' She paused, clearing her throat. 'Including sexually.'

'Good Lord, didn't the railways cure all that in the last century? Providing for wider intercourse?' asked Treasure too glibly. Watching her serious expression he added: 'Sorry. Not funny.'

'Didn't cure incest. Not so common now. Not restricted to rural areas, either. But you have it back there all right. Didn't see any menfolk except old Daras.'

'One could assume they were working in the fields.'

'Except there aren't any. Fields I mean. Or menfolk.' She sighed. 'The whole family's bonkers. Half-witted. You could see that. It's exactly what I'd been told about them. Daras was always a screw loose apparently. The others have got it from him in direct descent. And I mean direct.'

'Hence all the manic behaviour.'

'If you want to know, I'd guess that old man's been cohabiting with all the bedworthy women. And been doing it for years. Generations.'

'But why should the women submit to anything so degrading?'

'Broadly because they're all simple-minded and dependent on him. Easily put upon.'

'You knew that Ethel the sister and . . . and the other one, presumably a daughter, that they were unmarried?'

'Mm. There was a second daughter, that'd be Beryl. She left to get married. Which obviously didn't please her father.'

'And she had a daughter. Her husband died. Pounder seems

to have been involved with them. You don't know the husband's name?'

'No, but I can find out.'

'Clever of you to be so informed on the Dorset Horns and the . . . the . . .'

'The Frieslands? Keeping sheep for milk isn't so uncommon these days. They're a lot less trouble than cows, and far cheaper.'

'Well, I reckon your knowing about that got us in. And that dining room!' He shook his head incredulously.

'Some of the stuff was good?'

'Not just good. Magnificent. Most of it. I'd swear two of the landscapes were Constables. The big nymphs-and-shepherds canvas looked good sixteenth-century Italian. Possibly a Veronese. The silver was gorgeous. The furniture certainly worth a fortune.'

'Makes you wonder why the old boy's so hung up on money. Except . . .'

'If a recluse is hung up on money, it'd have to become a fix-ation. That and the prospect of making more money without parting with anything important.'

'You mean he'd sell a rough old Magna Carta copy but not his Constables?'

'That's about it. And could be just what he's been doing. Except the Magna Carta proved less rough than he first thought. 'Can't tell the difference,' he said. 'I wonder if he's right?'

'I don't see . . .'

'Neither did I, but I'm beginning to. He's sold one – the only one – I'd think for a great deal of money. To someone who he believes still has it. From whom he figured he could get it back. But that someone pretty certainly isn't Pounder.' Treasure fell silent after they had got over the gate to the road. 'You said Pounder and Daras were army friends. And stayed so after the war?'

'Not according to the locals. Daras dropped all outside con-tacts after his wife died.'

'But the family must have had some relations with the outside world. What about schooling, medical treatment, shopping? What about officialdom? The Inland Revenue, for heaven's sake? Government departments? Nobody gets away from them entirely. Life's too complicated. Too busy.' He looked for confirmation along the totally deserted highway, and, finding none, frowned at a grazing cow for not being a herd.

Glynis smiled. 'You can get away from a lot of things if you persevere. And deal with the rest by post. Plenty of country people never see a doctor.'

'And schooling? They don't do that by post. We're not in outer Mongolia.'

'I'd guess those girls had the minimum schooling. Like their mothers. Teachers don't complain if the class dimwit goes sick more often than anyone else. Plays truant more often. Leaves at the lowest permitted age.'

'Nobody would mind? Or care?' The tone was accusing.

'People – teachers and the like – would care up to a point. But that family is not just uninvolved. It's anti-social. They didn't just reject help. They spurned it. After a while people spurned them. All of them.'

'Tragic,' he exclaimed, taking her arm as they moved over the crossroads towards the car: it remained the only car in sight. 'But I'd still have thought they needed someone on the outside, as it were. An accountant or . . .' He stopped speaking and pointed ahead. 'Good Lord, I'd quite forgotten Hawker.' He quickened his pace. 'You all right?' he called.

The corporate investigator struggled up from where he'd been sitting on the wet verge beside the car. He made to come towards them but succeeded only in doing a sort of wobble on the spot. He was red around the eyes – as though he might have been crying. His clothes were dreadfully dishevelled. He was holding a shoe in one hand and he had been massaging an ankle with the other. Now he was standing on one leg. 'Think I'll survive,' he offered without conviction. 'Wanted to thank you. Much obliged for what you did. Saved my life.' He sighed deeply. 'Thought this must be your car. Wondered if you'd consider giving me a lift? Back to town?' He looked from one to the other. 'Terrible scare. Don't know why I came. Weak heart, you see?' Then slowly he sank again on to the verge.

'Of course we'll give you a lift,' said Glynis, dropping beside him. 'Twisted your ankle, have you? Let's have a look.'

Even Treasure, who didn't much care for Hawker, felt sorry for him. 'Don't believe you were in any real danger. It was sensible to get you out, though,' he said, watching Glynis's ministrations. 'Daras certainly seemed to have taken against you. But isn't that kind of thing in the normal line of work for a private detective?'

Hawker looked up, wheezing on the cigarette he had just lit. 'Very likely. But it's not my normal line of work. Betting-shop manager is what I am, Mr Treasure. Or was. Redundant, you see? Sleeping partner in Hawker & Bowles. But, like I told you, Bowles died. On Monday. Left me in a proper fix.'

'I see.' The banker's eyebrows lifted. 'Well, if we can get you in the car perhaps you'd like to tell us exactly what brought you to Litchester, and then out here? Take his other side, Glynis.'

'Not sure I can tell you that, Mr Treasure,' the other replied uncertainly.

'Well, I think it's time you tried,' said Treasure briskly. 'Come on.' He grasped one arm and tugged – a fraction before the girl was ready.

There was a tearing sound.

'Oh God!' whimpered Hawker, falling back on the swollen ankle, his other foot deeply embedded in the hem of his russet overcoat.

# Chapter Fourteen

Duggan squinted at the boiled kipper his wife had just set before him. Then, motionless, he continued to stare at his plate as though expecting the eyes in the divided fishhead to stare back in sympathy. He didn't at all enjoy kippers in the middle of the day, or at any other time for that matter, but he had given up saying so. Admitting he loathed what his wife gave him to eat on Fridays only enriched the vicarious satisfaction she took from being the instrument of his penance. He hoped that if he stopped complaining she might one day forget and give him something else. It was a forlorn hope, though – like the one about her accepting he'd been truly converted into the Church of England.

Bridget Duggan was still an old-fashioned Catholic. As far as she was concerned, her husband was only lapsed in the same faith and had enduring obligations. Although she had grown to suffer Mass in the English language, at least she could still ensure her family respected the fast days – as she was quite sure His Holiness the Pope did, too, whatever Father O'Connor said to the contrary.

'Is Rory not in yet?' Duggan frowned, focusing – with some difficulty – on the third place laid at the kitchen table. 'Isn't it two o'clock already?' The vergers worked a variable shift system. It was his month for late starting and finishing, with a two-hour lunch-break.

'It's twenty past two. You were late yourself,' she put in to forestall criticism of her favourite offspring. 'He went down to the Job Centre, looking for work.' So he could hardly be faulted by someone who had stayed too long in his favourite bar drinking too many Guinness and who was now half-asleep as a result. She sat down herself, bringing the teapot and her own plate over with her from the gas cooker.

'He wasn't long looking for work.' Duggan lowered his head, bringing it closer to his plate. He had begun tentatively separating fish from bone. 'Wasn't he at the cathedral trying to borrow five pounds from his poor old dad at noon?'

She sighed inwardly as she poured their tea. Rory had borrowed the same sum from her before he'd left at ten. 'Did you give it him?'

'I did not.'

'His dole money is precious little for a grown man to be living on.'

'Especially when he's the sole support of a dozen three-legged horses, not to mention a whole pack of bandy whippets.'

'That's not fair, Patrick. You might have helped him.' She was thinking of the winnings he'd owned to the night before.

'And who's going to help us when I'm put on the scrap heap? Which is any day now.' He filled his mouth with kipper and took a draught of the hot tea to help it down.

'But you've got Mr Pounder's job to go to when you retire. Before you retire. You said yesterday.' But there was already apprehension in her tone. 'Something's gone wrong?'

He swallowed hard. 'There'll be no Pounder job. I got the word from the Commander. Straight after matins this morning. He's sorry. It was a mistake. And not his only one,' he added darkly. 'He'd been ticked off by the Dean. I could tell that.'

'I said the Dean wouldn't approve.'

Duggan snorted. 'Been all right if I hadn't said I'd seen Canon Jones. I can tell you that. If I hadn't told the policeman. That's what did it all right. That and bloody Harry Jakes crawling again.'

'Well, they say he was promised the job. Not that he's going to need it at all. Not with all this money they're after coming into.'

'What money would that be?'

'Mr Pounder's. He's left thousands.'

'How many thousands?'

'That I don't know. Except it's a lot. And I got it from Mary

Saggs across the road, who's Harry Jakes's sister and ought to know. But we're not to say anything.' She drank some tea. 'And didn't you have to tell about Canon Jones? When you were asked?'

His glaze clouded. He hadn't had to tell about anyone. At the time of the police interview he'd been hung-over, as well as irritated with Canon Jones. 'Well, they'll not be looking to me to cover up for Pounder's paraffin heater. Not any more,' he asserted adamantly, and ignoring her question. 'And another thing: I haven't told all I saw. Not yet. I haven't said who else was there when I left last night.'

'Who was that?'

He adopted a look of sly caution. 'That's best kept to me own self for now, Mother.' Then when he saw her hurt expression he added: 'We don't want them troubling you for the information, do we?'

He was sorry already he'd brought up the subject and which he'd only done through vexation. This was the day she went to confession and he didn't trust that Father O'Connor. He wasn't going to risk having a negotiable confidence handed gratis to that loudmouth. Because wasn't that as good as sending the same intelligence for publication to the *Catholic Herald*, not to mention the *Police Gazette* – and all before he, Patrick Duggan, had even tested the market? He needed to see Commander Bliter again soon. He'd realised that with his fourth pint of Guinness. Maybe they'd change their minds on Pounder's job again if he hinted at what he hadn't told the police – not yet. It was a situation calling for extreme delicacy in the handling, of course.

'But how can they trouble me for information when they don't . . .'

'Sorry I'm late.' Rory sidled into the room. He still had on the black imitation leather jacket he wore outdoors. The back was streaked with mud. So were his trousers.

'You get terrible dirty sitting in that Job Centre,' sniggered his father.

'I slipped. Thanks, Mum.' Bridget Duggan had been quick to

fetch his kipper from the oven. 'Marvellous.' He smiled at her: kippers were his favourite.

'And where've you been, leaving your mother's cooking to spoil?' Duggan demanded sourly before beaming a sickly, ingratiating smile upon his wife.

'Couldn't help it.' Rory roughly pulled his chair in closer. The action rocked the table on which his father was resting both elbows while bringing his second, over-full cup of tea to his lips. What remained of Duggan's kipper was in consequence generously annointed with the hot liquid. 'Want to watch it, Dad,' said Rory quickly, believing always in taking the initiative. 'Say, did you see a short, fat guy in the cathedral this morning? With a bowler? Asking questions? I saw him after I spoke to you. Wanted to know about anyone called Daras.'

'So what if I saw him?' Duggan pushed away his big plate and reached for the cheese. 'You didn't give him anything?' It was nearly a point of honour with Duggan menfolk that so far as was humanly possible information of that sort was something paid for and never ever actually given away.

'Wasn't me he was asking. Not at first,' Rory answered carefully: he could be quite as devious as his father. 'Didn't know he'd been to you. Saw him talking to that young verger. Smith, is it? The one with acne? I was having a word with him later.'

'You weren't after borrowing money from Smith?' Duggan put in sharply and with inward deep concern. He usually owed Smith money himself.

''Course not. Him and me go to the same boozer. Play darts sometimes. We was just passing the time of day. Anyway, he says this character's wanting to trace a Daras. Ready to pay. Except Smith never hard of any Daras.'

'The man didn't say he was paying. Not when he asked me,' Duggan lied.

'Probably didn't want to insult you. 'Cos you look so bloody old and respectable. Well, I knew where a Daras lived. You showed me years ago. So I go after the guy. Catch him up at the Queen's Head. His name's Hawker.'

'And you gave him the information,' said Duggan in disgust.

'Something like that.'

'How much?'

'That's my business.'

Duggan disagreed. He'd stalled Hawker himself by telling him he'd make enquiries. Got him to leave his card. Told him to come back before evensong. He'd intended to go out to see Daras after lunch. Find out what it was worth not to give Hawker the Daras address. Then the whole thing had slipped his mind because of the other business with Bliter. Rory had most probably undercharged Hawker. On past performance Daras paid well for little services, and strictly on a business basis, too, because he and Duggan had stopped being friends years ago. Not so many people in the town had ever heard of the family nowadays. 'What happened after?' Duggan demanded.

'He took the bus out to Much Stratton and got shot at.'

'Go on?' said Duggan.

'You were there?' Rory's mother questioned in alarm.

'Not for long, I can tell you. Not after this crazy old man came up behind Hawker. In uniform he was. With a shotgun. Double-barrelled. Let it off right in Hawker's ear. Then stuck it in his back and marched him round the yard. That was when I come away.'

'Did Hawker know you were there?' asked the older Duggan.

'No. Nor any Daras, either. Only went out of curiosity. Got the same bus back after the shooting. Not taking chances.' He had been involved with the police a few months before, on suspicion of housebreaking, but there hadn't been enough evidence for a charge. Since then he'd avoided anything that could conceivably damage his entitlement to state welfare benefits. 'Crazy people. Must be. Tell you who was out there,' he put in as an afterthought, 'Glynis Jones.'

'Canon Jones's daughter?'

'That's right, Dad. Recognised her car. Soft-top Japanese job. Like a small Jeep. It was parked near the bus stop when I came back. Sure it was hers. She's a farm secretary.'

'Not for the Daras farm, she isn't,' said Duggan firmly. 'And keep out of her business. Stay right away from the cathedral clergy and their families. Daras, too, if you don't want more trouble.' He was already thinking of the money Pounder had left, putting two and two together, and wondering how he could get to Much Stratton and back before he was on duty again.

The Dean put down the telephone as his wife came into his study with a tea tray. 'That was Ewart Jones,' he said. 'He and his lawyer left the police station at two-thirty.'

'But it's nearly four now.'

'I know. He forgot to let me know.' He frowned, putting the braille sheets he had been reading into a drawer. 'Couldn't imagine why we were worried. You see, he just doesn't consider his position as at all serious.'

'And the fingerprint on the key?'

'He says the police seemed to accept he put it there the first time he attempted to get in and steal the Magna Carta,' he ended with a touch more acerbity.

'Don't you start talking that way. It's bad enough having Clive Brastow gunning for the Precentor.'

'Not to mention the wretched Duggan. I'm not gunning for Ewart. Just trying to get him to face the facts of the situation. If it hadn't been for Duggan, of course, Ewart need never have admitted that first visit.' He sniffed. 'Except, I suppose, he'd have owned up anyway. But there really is no call for cathedral servants to be volunteering other people's business to the police. Or interfering in mine,' he added with feeling. 'I've put a flea in Bliter's ear, I can tell you.'

'Poor Commander Bliter. Perhaps his wife unnerves him. She does me. This was over Duggan?'

'Certainly. Damned impudence overriding Jakes's claim to Pounder's job. At least he should have consulted me first. Frankly, I find the whole business sinister. Chap reeks of booze all the time.'

'Bliter?'

'No, Duggan. You must have noticed. Booze or peppermint.'

'Not everyone has your acute sense of smell, darling.'

'Well, you can't have the Dean's verger blowing alcohol fumes at all the communicants.'

'As senior verger he must be doing it at all the tourists.'

'That's different. Only slightly, I admit. And anyway he's retiring soon. Not to be resurrected in another guise. Not while I'm Dean.'

Margaret Hitt looked at her watch. 'Dr Welt is late. Shall I pour your tea?' As she spoke the doorbell rang. 'Ah, that'll be him.'

A few minutes later Welt was sitting on the edge of the chair in front of the Dean's desk looking vulnerable. Mrs Hitt had retired to her workroom.

'Donald, I asked if you could call . . .'

'It's about my job? Winding down the musical establishment? I thought with the insurance money for the Magna Carta we'd be OK.' The words came with a rush.

'I've no idea. Not yet. And that certainly wasn't why I wanted to see you. Something much more delicate.'

The other man stiffened. 'My relationship with Miss Larks . . .' He stopped, cursing himself for anticipating again. It was exactly what he'd determined to avoid before the interview, except it was not in his nature. And the Dean disarmed him. He could cope with anyone else, even bully them. The Dean was different.

'Your relations with Miss Larks are entirely your own business and hers,' Hitt put in blandly. 'It's about your movements last evening.'

'I don't understand. I've already told the police where I was.'

'That's the trouble. Someone says they saw you going into the cathedral at six-thirty. By the cloister door.' The Dean leaned back in his chair. 'It's something you're alleged not to have mentioned to the police. I imagine it wouldn't be appropriate for that someone to do so?'

'No, it wouldn't. I mean . . .' He loosened his collar. 'This is stupid. Telling the police would only complicate things. To absolutely no purpose. Who's saying this? Who saw me?'

'Does it matter? So much as whether it's true? In a way you

could say it's someone who's perjured themselves for you already if it is true. I mean by not telling the police.' The other man paused, frowning. 'Perhaps that's putting it too strongly.' He was thinking of what he'd said to his wife earlier as he went on: 'I am not of the view we're obliged to indict each other when it comes to volunteering information to the police. Might be different if one were under oath. In a court of law. Not everyone takes that view, of course,' he ended, more reflectively than pointedly.

Welt leant even further forward in his chair, elbows on his knees, fists clenched hard. 'All right. I did go into the cathedral. At about six-thirty. Force of habit. Did whoever saw me say I also came out again? Straight away?'

'No. Did you?'

'But if I was being watched I must have been seen coming out again,' he said slowly, concentrating his gaze on the Dean's face, and hanging on his reaction.

'I don't think you were being watched. You were simply seen to go in. If you came out again immediately and are prepared to swear as much to me, I'd tell the person concerned just that. And I'd expect your word, our word to be accepted. You say it was force of habit?'

'Most week-nights just recently I've been having supper at a Chinese restaurant. The one at the top of Bridge Street. Last night I decided to go back to the Italian place in Talbot Court. At the far end of East Street. It's where I used to go regularly. Different direction of course.'

'You mean when you went to Bridge Street you'd go through the cathedral?'

'Because it's quicker. Yesterday I'd gone through the cloister door before remembering I was heading the wrong way. Thinking of something else at the time. Anyway, I came out again before I'd even shut the door behind me.'

'Locked it?'

'No, because I hadn't had to unlock it.'

'I'd forgotten. That came up before. Pounder hadn't left, so it wasn't locked.'

'It often wasn't. Not at half past six. Pounder was often still around then. He'd usually locked the north door, though.'

'It's easier for you to go through the cathedral if you're going to Bridge Street? Even if you have to unlock and relock a door on the way? Sometimes two doors? With cumbersome locks?'

The organist relaxed a little. 'In the daytime it's quicker. With no locking to do. At suppertime recently it's just been less . . . embarrassing.'

'I'm sorry, I don't follow.'

'Sounds ridiculous, but it was a ruse. To avoid meeting someone. A few weeks ago when I was making for Talbot Court I was waylaid too often.' He affected an especially stern expression before remembering this could hardly impress his blind companion.

'You were waylaid? Good heavens.'

'By a lady. One we both know. It was always made to look like coincidence. Because she comes home that way. So she said. But I think she waited for me. I know she did.'

'Every night?'

'Too many for it actually to be coincidence.'

'And you're a creature of habit. I mean she knew what time . . . ?'

'I have a routine, yes.'

'And this lady studied it? To what purpose?'

'To invite me to supper. At her place. Pretending the whole thing was spontaneous. But always on nights when I think she knew she'd be alone – either the whole evening or because we'd be left by ourselves after the meal.' He looked at the telephone, which had started to ring while he'd been speaking. 'D'you want to answer that?'

Hitt shook his head. 'My wife will take it.' The ringing stopped as he spoke. 'Tell me if I'm being naïve, but why couldn't the lady invite you to dine in the normal way? By letter or on the telephone?'

'She did. Frequently. I went once. Never again. I'd rather not go into the reasons.' He made the last statement sound deeply significant. 'Anyway, she'd given up asking me formally, in advance – when I could plead another engagement, or back out later.'

'I see. Also why you'd go to some pains to avoid these meetings. But the waylaying's stopped? You mentioned you'd reverted to . . .'

'Because I'm afraid I was rude to the lady earlier this week. She won't be inviting me any more.' He paused before adding with evident venom: 'It's also why she's been snooping on me. Aiming to get me into trouble with you and the police.' He inhaled sharply. 'It is Olive Merit we've been talking about, of course.'

'Oh dear . . .' began the Dean, just as the door opened and Margaret Hitt appeared.

'I'm sorry to interrupt, but it's important. Ursula Brastow's in hospital. In a coma. It seems she's tried to take her life. An overdose of barbiturates. She left a note saying Mark Treasure would explain. They're trying to find him. He's not due here, is he?'

# Chapter Fifteen

It was five-fifteen when Olive Merit crossed the school yard to the gate. Despite the strong wind blowing in her face, her head was up and her stride bold. She pulled the light brown topcoat tightly around her, clasping the bulging briefcase close to her unbulging bosom.

The Chancellor's sister had a car of her own but she seldom brought it to school. She preferred to walk to and from her work in all weathers. It was less than ten minutes to the house.

She taught speech and drama to the senior school – boys and girls, but most of the takers were girls aged sixteen to eighteen. Half the sessions were voluntary and normally took place after regular school hours. But Friday was one of her early evenings, and tonight she was in an especial hurry. She had the drinks party to prepare.

''Scuse me, Miss Merit. Can I have a word?' The short, dumpy woman who had been waiting outside by the street lamp was middle-aged and unseasonably dressed in clothes too young for her. The tight skirt of her flimsy cotton dress finished well above her knees and well below the shiny black jacket. Her hair was an unreal reddish colour and she wore a great deal of make-up. She wobbled forward in clattering high-heeled shoes.

'Hello, Mrs Larks. Good to see you,' said Miss Merit in a heartier tone and with a warmer sentiment than she felt was justified – but she tried not to harbour grudges. 'You looking for me? Something I can do? How's Cindy?'

'Well, that's it, see? She's gone off. Disappeared like,' replied

Mrs Larks, normally a gossipy, loquacious woman but for the moment conscious that drama would be heightened by brevity.

'She hasn't been with you?'

'I haven't seen her. But I know she was about yesterday. Surely she can't have disappeared?'

'Eleven o'clock this morning they came for her. Police I thought they was. 'Cept I got it wrong. They was from the lawyers. I'd just come in from work. I do cleaning in the mornings. Well, Cindy wasn't in of course. At work. At the shop she was. They didn't know where she worked. Only about her being in the cathedral choir. So I phoned the shop and spoke to her. We're on the phone now. Told her these men was wanting to see her.'

'The lawyers?' Miss Merit put in shortly, while motioning the other woman to fall into step beside her: it really was too cold to be standing about, and in any case she had no time to waste.

'That's right. Except I said they was police. Like today, first thing.'

'You had real police round this morning?'

Mrs Larks sniffed hard and adjusted the white, wet-look handbag that dangled from her shoulder on a long strap. 'Thought they'd never go. One of them took a fancy to Cindy. You could see that. Her in her shorty dressing gown, too.' There was unmistakable envy in the tone. She tried to lengthen her step to match Miss Merit's, failed in that attempt, and reverted to the tiptoe gait that came out closer to a foxtrot than it did to a walk.

Two of Miss Merit's pupils cycled passed. Both cast quizzical looks at Mrs Larks. 'Good night, Miss Merit. Have a nice weekend.'

'Good night, Alice. Good night, Poppy.' She waved to the girls. 'So why did the lawyers want Cindy?'

'About Mr Pounder. You know, the one who died last night? Left her a lot of money, he has. So they said.'

'Did you tell Cindy this?'

''Course I did. And I said she'd better stay where she was. They was coming round to see her.' Now she was breathing quite heavily. 'And that's the last anyone's seen of her. Could we slow up a bit?'

'Sorry.' Miss Merit slackened the pace, then had to increase it again as she led the way over a controlled pedestrian crossing. You didn't mention how much money?'

'Didn't know how much. They didn't tell me.' She transferred her bag to the other shoulder and pulled up her skirt a fraction to improve her stride. 'I told her it was a lot, though. Then she hung up on me.'

'And left the shop?'

'Straight away, the manageress told me. And she never went to the cathedral this afternoon. I just been there.'

'You mean she didn't turn up for evensong?'

'That's right. And not for the practice they had before, neither.'

'Have you asked the organist if he's seen her? Dr Welt?' Her lips closed after the question, then tightened.

'No. Why should I? I asked Mr Duggan, the verger. He hadn't seen her.' Her toe caught in a paving stone and she staggered ahead of her companion, very nearly falling over.

'Careful.' Miss Merit took the other's arm. 'Well, I think it's early to be talking about a disappearance. I mean, from what you say she's only been gone a few hours. Probably needed to think something out.'

'Not like her, it isn't. Blame meself, I do. For getting the message wrong. I didn't mean to say they was from the law.'

'Well, there's no reason why Cindy should want to escape from the police, even if she did misunderstand you. There has to be a logical explanation. She's not a silly girl, and she's old enough to know her own mind.' And it hadn't been her fault that she'd had to leave school two years before. Miss Merit blamed the mother for that, robbing the child of a great future – and robbing Olive Merit of the chance to create a promising star turn.

'It's the money. You don't think she'll lose the money? Not being here to claim it?' The questions were more searching than the others, more evidently the real reason for Mrs Larks's concern.

'Of course she won't lose it. But she's eighteen now. Of age.

143

You know it'll be her money?' The question was put almost threateningly.

Money had been the reason for the abrupt finish to Cindy's formal education. Mrs Larks had claimed she couldn't afford to maintain her daughter at school. When Miss Merit herself had offered to contribute substantially to the costs for two years both women had turned her down – Cindy because she was too proud, the mother because she wanted Cindy out earning her keep. And, in the process, Olive Merit had somehow forfeited the affection of the child. That affection she sensed had now been transferred to Donald Welt. His ambitious plans for Cindy's future she regarded as a blind: she was convinced he was only really after the girl's body.

'I'm only thinking of Cindy. I wouldn't want her deprived of her rights,' whined Mrs Larks self-righteously.

'I've told you there's no fear of that,' Miss Merit countered briskly, dropping the other's arm, bridling at the hypocrisy and shuddering involuntarily because she had just thought of Donald Welt. 'It can't be all that much money. Mr Pounder couldn't have been rich.'

'Richer than anyone thought. Is what the lawyers said. That's why they wanted to talk to Cindy. Before anyone else like.'

'Like whom?'

'They didn't say. Not outright. The police I thought they meant. He was murdered.' She paused, mostly for breath. 'Foul play being suspected like,' she added earnestly. 'He was a friend of ours.'

'I see,' said Miss Merit, who was now beginning to. 'I suppose Cindy can't have gone to her grandfather?'

'Never. Wouldn't have her. He don't recognise her, see? She's a Larks to him. Not a Daras.'

Mark Treasure guided the Dean of Litchester through the crowded polished hall of the hospital towards the exit. Detective Chief Inspector Pride was with them.

'You think Mrs Brastow will survive?' asked the Dean. 'It was difficult to ask with her husband there. D'you think we should be leaving him like this?'

'The doctor says the chances are good.' It was Pride who answered. 'She'll probably stay in a coma for another day, though. He told me it was a serious attempt. Not a sham like they are sometimes – a craving for attention, if you follow me? Better to let the Canon stay for a bit. He'll come away later.'

The others were conscious the policeman was speaking with the special assurance born of experience. They were relieved at his view while neither of them at all envied a calling that produced such a tutored insight.

'It's an impressive intensive care unit,' offered Treasure.

'All the support services you could want,' Pride confirmed in a distinctly proprietorial way. 'My wife works here. In the physiotherapy department. It's a good hospital.'

'Dreadful thing to have done. Whoops!' exclaimed the Dean as Treasure brought them both to an abrupt halt. 'What did we just miss?'

'Sorry. A trolley with a patient on it. In a hurry. Place is like a railway station.'

'Airport I always think, sir,' said Pride in a matter-of-fact tone. 'Of course it's visiting time. Always more crowded. Christmas coming, too.' He cleared his throat and came closer to the others. 'Pity we hadn't known she was into psychoanalysis.'

'Her husband didn't till today,' countered the Dean. 'Would it have made any difference?'

They passed through the electrically operated doors on to a roofed concourse outside. Pride drew them aside away from the mainstream of human traffic. 'It was the trick cyclist who gave her the barbiturates,' he observed with heavy emphasis.

'Who'd have believed she'd have tried taking her life because she wrote me a letter? Even if she is neurotic,' Treasure said, aiming to steer the conversation away from the direction he figured the policeman was taking it. 'All she'd done was try to nobble me. But in a really quite inoffensive way.'

'If I could have the details of that now, sir?' Pride had produced a notebook.

'Sure. She wrote to me about three weeks ago. Said she understood I intended voting against the sale of the Magna Carta. Which was quite true then. She begged I wouldn't change my mind . . .'

'*Begged,* sir?'

'That was the word she used, as I remember.'

'Thanks. Go on, please.'

'Well, she explained who she was. How important it was the thing shouldn't be sold, even though her husband was in favour of selling. That was the odd part.' Treasure frowned. It was a rum letter and, I have to admit, one I treated as having very little consequence. At the time. Different now.'

'Has to be what she meant in the suicide note, sir. That you would explain. Did she say anything else in the letter?'

'Not that I recall. Oh, she didn't want her husband to know she'd written, which, incidentally, seemed reasonable.'

'You still have the letter?' This was the Dean.

'Yes. It'll be on file at the office.'

'Did you reply to it, sir?' asked Pride.

'No. Because she specifically asked me not to.'

'Didn't want to risk Clive Brastow opening it probably,' said the Dean.

'I'd meant to refer to her letter if I met her alone. And I did meet her this morning. But the opportunity passed for some reason. Oh, I remember now. Some-one else joined us. Then quite thoughtlessly I admitted in the lady's hearing that I'd changed my mind. About the sale. That was when her husband was with us.'

'Did she seem to take it badly?' the Dean enquired slowly.

'Didn't appear to. Now I suppose she must have done. Possibly thought it was the letter made me switch sides. In a contrary kind of way. That would have been indefensible, of course.'

The policeman looked up from his note-taking, his normally dour expression deepened by the banker's firm disclaimer. 'The letter didn't affect your view, sir?'

'Afraid it didn't. Not one way or the other. Frankly it seemed an irrelevance at the time. And it certainly didn't impress a life-or-death decision was involved.' He made a loud tutting sound which caused two passing ambulance men to look at him as though they'd been accused of something. 'Obviously, I didn't know she was in a chronic nervous state.' The men glanced at each other as they moved away, one shaking his head.

'Her husband said to her he might have to resign if the Magna Carta was sold, sir. He just told me that. But it was right he was in favour of the sale himself of course. The Dean's sure of that.'

'And I've given you the explanation, Mr Pride. Canon Brastow supported the sale on condition the funds weren't spent on the cathedral but went to overseas Christian aid.' The Dean shrugged. 'I'm afraid he wouldn't have got his way. He knew it, too. We all did.'

'Which explains why his wife didn't want the thing sold at all, Chief Inspector,' said Treasure.

'Also why she might have thought making a secret plea over anything so important was a wicked thing for her to have done, sir.'

'Wicked.' The Dean gave an interested smile as he repeated the policeman's word.

'Accepting that the shame at having sent the letter to Mr Treasure was what really drove her to this, sir.'

'She left a note that seemed to say so, Mr Pride.'

'That's as may be, sir. But now we know she was in possession of barbiturates. That alters things, you see? We have to consider whether it was she who might have drugged Mr Pounder's tea. Or worse. That's in view of her subsequent actions.' Pride wasn't taking notes any more. He was blatantly watching the reactions of the others to this very incautious speculation.

'That would be a quite unsupportable postulation,' commented the Dean firmly but without emotion. 'It'd be like . . .' He hesitated, then continued. 'Well, you know it's now common knowledge that Pounder died a comparatively rich man . . .'

'Is it?' Treasure interrupted, surprised.

'I was told as much in strict confidence. By three separate informants in the course of today.' The Dean smiled wrily. 'You've heard obviously, Mr Pride?'

'Yes, sir. Also that someone's been talking out of turn.'

'The point is,' continued the Dean, 'it'd be quite as credible, though no more practicably tenable, to suppose Pounder's death was caused by someone likely directly to gain from it. That certainly wouldn't involve the wife of a member of the cathedral chapter.' He wiped a hand over his forehead. 'That's a red herring, of course, Mr Pride. But no redder than your barbiturate theory. Ursula Brastow couldn't possibly have been involved in murder.'

'I take your point, sir,' said the policeman, but without an inflection to indicate he was anywhere near accepting it. 'Happens one of the alleged beneficiaries of Mr Pounder's will has disappeared.'

'A member of the family?' the Dean asked quickly.

'Miss Cindy Larks. Eighteen. Senior girl chorister in the cathedral, I believe?'

'That's right, Mr Pride.'

'Specially friendly with Dr Welt, the organist. Or so we understand.'

'And to whom do you owe that understanding?'

Treasure was impressed by the Dean's spirited question as well as the evident sense of loyalty that had prompted it.

'Dr Welt himself, really, sir.' The policeman was unchastened by the suggestion of rebuff. 'He can't account for her absence, but she has a date with him at seven-fifteen this evening. At his house. For a singing lesson. She hasn't been seen since eleven this morning.'

'And Pounder's left her money? They were friends?' This was Treasure.

'We're looking into that, sir. Seems they must have been.'

'Someone's reported her missing?' the Dean asked.

'Her mother, sir.'

The clergyman fingered his watch. 'But it's only just after five-thirty now. Isn't she a bit elderly to be reported missing by her mother after so short a time?'

'We thought the same, sir. Mrs Larks came to the station just after five apparently. Uniformed sergeant on duty told me just now, when I was leaving to come here. The mother mentioned the connection with Mr Pounder.'

'Over-anxious but commendably concerned for her daughter, I expect,' said the Dean.

'Worried about the money, the sergeant said, sir. Wouldn't stop talking about it.'

# Chapter Sixteen

Duggan had made sure the cathedral was empty before he let himself out through the cloister door, locking it behind him.

The police had left at midday. The north door had been in use again and the routine was more or less back to normal, except that the Old Library was closed.

It's true it was now only five-forty, earlier than the building was supposed to be secured, but Duggan had persuaded himself that without the Magna Carta there was no reason why the place should be kept open after evensong in midwinter. Probably the rules would be changed officially before long, making life easier for him when he was finally confirmed in his appointment as Dean's verger – an office he was once again confident of securing. Meantime, since there was no one about, he was making his own rules for today because he had other benefits pending that needed his urgent attention.

Hunching his shoulders inside the heavy black overcoat with the extra lining, once the property of a now deceased archdeacon, and pulling the worn Homburg over his forehead, Duggan rounded the Lady Chapel, then headed west along the close, muttering to himself. He was taking a different from normal route. The dark figure in the shadows registered this, at first with annoyance, then with calculated approval, before falling in quietly some way behind.

When he reached Bridge Street the verger turned left. He looked over his shoulder, but not carefully enough to spot he was being followed. He was making for the Jakes house on the far side of the river. It had been a reflex action to check whether anyone might be watching. He wasn't apprehensive. Simply his conscience was sensitive – not pricked.

The business shouldn't take long, but it wouldn't wait – not if he was to make certain of getting Pounder's job. Jakes would be ready enough to pass it up when he heard that Duggan knew the source of old Pounder's legacy: well, guessed the source of it at least. He gave the long woollen scarf another turn around his neck. It was much colder tonight. 'Colder,' he said aloud to himself, for there was no one within hearing.

The street was nearly empty. Very little through traffic came that way since the new, high bridge had been built two hundred yards up-river to link with the outer ring road. There were no shops with lighted windows in Bridge Street south of the close, and the pavement narrowed where the road dipped beside the Bishop's Palace. It wasn't much wider on the other side where a mixed row of refurbished eighteenth-century houses made an attractive terrace. It was on this side that the other figure was now moving, close to the houses, unobserved in the shadows, though nearly parallel to the pursued.

Duggan was pleased with himself for having gone to see Daras. He'd got a lift in a lorry to Much Stratton and caught the bus back. He'd been late returning for duty but there'd been no one to notice. He'd had trouble getting into the Daras house, but he'd expected that, and Daras was being a lot more receptive when he'd left. He'd known how to treat Joshua Daras, another erstwhile friend. You had to realise he told you more in the things he wouldn't say than in the things he did say: in a manner of speaking – or, rather, not speaking. Duggan chuckled at his own joke.

There were no lights on the bridge, only reinstated gas lamps at either end which had replaced the universally deplored sodium lights installed in the 1950s. The narrow five-arched medieval bridge was a gem of its kind, splendidly intact and much admired, even though the pavements were too mean to accommodate two walkers abreast. Duggan was unaffected by the aesthetic charm of the structure. He stumbled in the bad light as he stepped onto it.

'Damned kerb,' he complained aloud, dropping the good humour and peering ahead with narrowed gaze.

The bridge was deserted on both sides in front of him. A van swept too close from behind, reminding him to stay well in on the pavement. When he was halfway across the swollen river a motor-cycle surged into view from the south. The rider roared over the bridge with headlamp on high beam, swerved maliciously at Duggan and temporarily blinded him.

'Rotten bastard,' exclaimed the verger in what was to be his last ever coherent utterance, for it was at that moment that the figure dogging him seized the looked-for opportunity, ran across the empty road, placed both hands in the small of Duggan's back, and pushed him hard over the less than waist-high and much admired medieval parapet.

Duggan couldn't swim, and in any case the heavy coat and the freezing, rushing water made effective movement impossible. He was too astonished to cry out as he fell, and soon he was too full of water – not that there had been anyone to hear. He was dis-covered quite soon afterwards by someone walking his dog on the river bank, which was well illuminated a bit further on. But Duggan was very dead by then, attached to a mooring post by his long scarf.

Margaret Hitt had been admitted to the New Library some min-utes after the despatch of the head verger. Seeing the lights on still, she said, she had stopped in for a private word, and hoped she wasn't interrupting anything.

'Not at all,' Laura Purse offered brightly but appearing some-what flushed. She motioned the Dean's wife to the visitor's chair. 'I've been out. Came back to clear up a few things. Mostly done now. Thought I'd hang on here till it's time for the Merits' sherry party. It's hardly worth going home.'

'That's because you're always so band-box. And young and attractive with it, of course. I shall have to go home first to repair facial ravages and put on something showier.' Mrs Hitt sighed, plucked at her tweed coat and made a self-deprecating grimace.

'You've been to the hospital?'

'Mm. Quite early on. Ursula Brastow will survive. But that's not what I came to talk about. I think Gerard Twist is one of the most agreeable young men I know,' the older woman continued firmly and now in a getting-down-to-business tone. 'Strong in spirit and with a refreshing air of . . .'

'Unworldliness?' the librarian supplied carefully and with a hint of caution showing in her eyes.

'I'm sure that's right. You know him so much better than I. An exceptional man, with a splendid musical talent. I've always been concerned that people might take advantage of his good nature. That he's a sort of innocent at large.'

'I expect to marry him. Are you here to protect him? To warn me off?' The gaze was perfectly steady, like the voice.

'Oh, my dear, quite the opposite. Now, why should you have thought that?'

Laura gave a relieved smile. 'I don't know. Because I'm on my guard, perhaps? You're worried for Gerard's well-being. His mother's not wild about me. I thought she might have recruited you against me.'

'Never met his mother. Expect she's overfond of him. Most mothers would be. Anyway, in future I shall take greater care about how I express things. Must be getting careless. Probably my age. Almost certainly my age.' She sniffed. 'When did he ask you – to marry him?'

'He hasn't yet. But he will. When I'm ready.' The big eyes opened especially wide in a gesture of what could still have been defiance.

'And you'll accept him?'

'Certainly. I'm very fond of him. And he needs looking after.'

'I hope you'll stay in Litchester.'

'Not much doubt of that. Provided Gerard's job holds up.'

'I'm sure it will.' Mrs Hitt paused, looked seriously perplexed, then continued. 'Also I'm sure Gerard has the interests of the cathedral very much at heart.'

'We both do.'

'One shouldn't allow a . . . a misadventure . . . an upset to mar things. In any circumstances.'

It was Laura's turn to look puzzled. 'I don't really know what you mean.'

'So please indulge me by hearing me out. Tell me, did you both know last evening that the Magna Carta would probably be sold?'

Laura shook her head. 'No, we didn't. We understood quite the opposite.'

'I thought as much. For those of us who were thinking that way but dearly wanted the thing sold . . .'

'Like us? Gerard and me?'

'Precisely. For us the fire came as a blessing. Don't you think? In a way? Apart from poor Mr Pounder's death, of course. Incidentally, did you know he wasn't at all poor in the material sense? Or so it seems. Well, there it is.' She went on without waiting for a reply to her question. 'The fact is the fire provided a sort of reprieve – the insurance money being almost as good as a sale.'

'Except now everybody knows the Chapter would have voted for selling.'

'Now we know. We didn't then. Which means any one of us could have considered starting that fire.'

'But not murdering Pounder? That'd be far-fetched, surely?'

'And what if his death was really an accident?'

'But how could it? He was hit on the head.'

'There are accidents and accidents,' said Mrs Hitt in a tone that firmly defied challenge.

'You mean . . . he might somehow have got in the way?'

'Something of the kind. It's hard to believe any sane person knowingly meant to kill such a harmless old man.'

'Not some tearaway even?'

'Possibly. And if it was one of those it'll most probably stay an unsolved crime. When there's no motive, you see, it must be difficult for the police. Meantime, it's very tiresome for a person to be put under suspicion through another person's uncorroborated and possibly vague testimony.'

'I still don't follow.'

'Simpletons court celebrity, and that applies to simpletons of all backgrounds and social levels. Litchester's alive with them. This morning I had someone asking whether some tittle tattle should be retailed to the police. Someone who really should have known better. Then coming out of evensong just now that oily fellow Duggan bearded me. He wanted to know if he should tell the police there was someone other than Canon Jones he saw when he was leaving the cathedral last night. Around six-thirty. Someone important, he said.'

'Why should he ask you?'

'Said he'd intended to ask my husband, who wasn't at the service. I imagine he's up to ingratiating himself with us by pretending he values our advice. So that he gets Mr Pounder's job. There's not a chance. Gilbert simply loathes him. You won't mention that to anybody?'

'Of course not. So what did you tell Duggan?'

'That he should follow his conscience and the Beatitudes. That flummoxed him, I can tell you. That's not the point, though.' Mrs Hitt shifted in her chair. 'I hear two of the choristers thought they saw Gerard in North Street at a . . . at an inconvenient time last evening? At twenty to seven?'

'And they got it wrong. He and I were at my flat before then.' The words came with belligerent sharpness.

'I don't think schoolboy testimony matters much, but I believe mine would. If Duggan should claim it was Gerard he saw, I'm very happy to witness he couldn't have.'

Laura looked surprised. 'Duggan didn't say it was Gerard?'

'Didn't say who it was. I never gave him the chance. The point is I was ringing your doorbell at six-twenty last night.' The Dean's wife capped the utterance with a look of great satisfaction.

The librarian coloured slightly. 'I don't remember . . . We couldn't have . . .'

'Heard the bell? Of course you couldn't,' the other emphasised. 'Something much more important than doorbells being played. One of the Brandenburg Concertos. The Third, I think. Fairly thumping away on your record-player up there. Could hear it quite clearly from the street. I wonder the neighbours don't complain. '

The girl grimaced. 'They do occasionally.'

'I didn't ring twice. Shouldn't have rung at all once I twigged I'd be intruding, but I was passing and wanted to borrow a book. Don't need it now. Anyway, I saw Gerard. He had his back to your kitchen window.'

'To be honest, I'm not absolutely sure of the time he arrived. Not the exact time. Not to the minute,' Laura offered carefully. She studied the other's face.

'Well, if necessary I'll swear you were both there at six-twenty. Don't suppose it will be necessary. But it might stop other people putting silly times to Gerard's movements. I'm not the easiest person to contradict. And I have an extremely reliable watch.'

Laura leant forward, her forearms resting on the desk top, hands clasped. 'You don't have to do this.' She was trying to make up her mind whether Mrs Hitt was genuinely mistaken about the time of her visit to North Street or whether she was deliberately offering to perjure herself.

'One does what one sees as right, my dear,' the Dean's wife observed, offering no answer to the unspoken questions. 'I'm hardening to the view the crime was committed by what you call a tearaway. The sooner the police do the same, the sooner we'll all be left in peace. Until then we must all do our best to support each other's interests.'

'But since we didn't see you last night.' Now it was dawning on the girl that a *quid pro quo* arrangement might be intended. 'I mean, you must have been . . .'

'At large at the critical time? Don't worry about me. I'm well enough alibi'd. And, in any case, deans' wives are traditionally above suspicion.' She began to do up her coat.

'I suppose Pounder's death wasn't in vain?' asked Laura.

'Not at all in vain. And finding whoever brought it about may prove a minor triumph for justice, but it won't bring him back. Meantime the cathedral is a million pounds to the good. Perhaps directly due to Mr Pounder.' She paused in her purposeful actions while allowing a finger to trace the outline of her cheek. 'Do you suppose a police enquiry could in any circumstances be called an administrative sophistry?'

'I'm sorry?'

'No, I'm sure it couldn't.' The brief visionary look had matched the softened tone. Mrs Hitt shook her head sharply, then rose from the chair with a confident sigh. 'Well, that's done. I must fly, but I'll see you again shortly. Tell Gerard we talked. It's important he knows where he stands. Where you both stand.'

# Chapter Seventeen

Treasure replaced the telephone in the Dean's study. 'The evening telephonist at the Red Dragon thinks it was a woman who left me the message last night.'

'The one about Daras.' The Dean nodded from the small drinks table behind the desk. 'Only sherry here. Amontillado. Like some? Or I can get you the Scotch from the drawing room?'

'Sherry's fine. Thank you. Shall I pour it?'

But his host was already doing so – precisely, with a liquid-level indicator, a small ball which he balanced in turn on the edges of the glasses. The device had two metal prongs of different lengths protruding from it to calculate short or long drinks. 'It's electronic. Makes a bleep when I've given us enough,' Hitt explained. 'Takes some of the fun out of life, but also reduces wastage.'

The two men had been delivered to the Deanery in the Chief Inspector's car. This was the first time they had been able to converse alone since meeting at the hospital. Treasure had joined Hitt there in response to a message from Mrs Hitt.

'You don't know this woman's identity?' The Dean placed a glass and coaster on the desk in front of Treasure, then settled himself in his leather swivel chair.

'Unfortunately, no. I do know she was steering me to the source of the Magna Carta copy. Can't be much doubt of that. You'd never heard of the Daras family?'

'Not that I recall. We're still comparative newcomers here, of course. Eight years. But, from what you've said already, our ignorance does us credit.' He took a sip of his drink. 'Interesting that Pounder knew Daras. Fits with his telling me there were Magna Carta copies to be had in the area.'

'How long ago did he tell you that?'

'Hard to remember. Five, six years. Certainly more than four. Does it matter?'

'It could be significant. I'd better tell you the rest of what happened at Much Stratton this afternoon.'

A few minutes later the Dean was shaking his head in continuing surprise as he said: 'And did this Hawker chap come clean on the way back?'

'Nearly. He was hired to come here and check the authenticity of our Magna Carta.'

'By whom?'

'That he still won't say. He leads one to assume it's the American bidder. Except he's such an unlikely agent for a respectable museum.'

'He's not a specialist in some aspect of antiquarian scholarship?'

Treasure chuckled. 'I'd forgotten you haven't met him. He used to work in a betting shop. Now unemployed and the sleeping partner in what I suppose you'd call a detective agency. Unfortunately for him, the working partner just died. He wasn't a scholar, either. Ex-policeman. Good at the job, or so Hawker insists.'

'How did he die? He wasn't killed?'

'Nothing sinister. Burst appendix, poor chap. Hawker felt obliged to take over the current work. Seems to have arrived here with very little to go on. He did know I'd come to Litchester, and he picked up the Daras lead from reading my message at the hotel last night.'

'Which he pinched?'

'No. He was handed it by mistake. Gave it back after noting the contents. He got the Daras address from a fellow in a pub. Probably Duggan the verger's son. I told you he was out there, too?'

'Mm. But you don't know why.'

'Glynis Jones says he's naturally into other people's business.'

The Dean snorted. 'Like his father.'

'Hawker went to Much Stratton, he admitted, because he had no other lead. I think he came to regret that.'

'And where does a Magna Carta copy come into all this?'

'It doesn't at the moment. Not unless one attaches importance to the miserable Hawker and his mission, and the ravings of the unmentionable Daras. There may have been a trade in fake Magna Cartas at some time, but I don't see its significance in relation to the fire.' The banker paused, then continued half to himself: 'Not unless, of course . . .'

'I'm still perplexed.' The Dean had not intended to interrupt but since he had, and thereafter continued speaking, he had the effect of delaying Treasure's fresh train of deductive thought by about an hour. 'No one could have wanted the Magna Carta destroyed for personal gain,' the Dean went on. 'But no one who cared deeply enough about the cathedral to be going for the insurance money could have contemplated murdering Pounder. In the main we're talking of devout clerics. Or their equally devout womenfolk.'

'None of whom would rate a clergyman's job as more important than Pounder's life? No, of course not,' Treasure answered his own question but without really deep-sounding conviction.

'Oh, it's possible in theory,' came the Dean's bland rejoinder. 'We have potential martyrs amongst us.' He sniffed at his sherry while evidently considering the candidates. 'Martyrs basically have to dismiss the significance of this life on earth. In theory, I suppose, they might feel justified in applying the same dictum to other people's lives. In a sound cause. In practice, though, none of the clergy jobs here is really at risk.'

'The Minor Canon . . . ?'

'Twist? He might have felt the need to move on. Yes, we might even have had to encourage him to. In certain circumstances. But I can't see such a mild fellow taking a life in order to protect his livelihood. Nor even the Litchester musical tradition. Not sure that applies to Welt, of course.'

'That's the fiery organist you were interviewing this afternoon? Who gives the missing Cindy Larks singing lessons.'

The Dean nodded. 'Curious chap. Pretty good musician. Better perhaps than we deserve for what we can pay. Not that the Lord doesn't deserve the best, and fortunately there's a glut of good organists at the moment. Welt is also a developing composer, which is good for our public relations.'

'But he has what you termed a tiresome private life.'

'Yes. Ruthless in that connection, I'd say. *He's* not in holy orders of course. Nor is he a professing Christian.' The Dean stopped speaking but his deepening expression indicated he hadn't stopped counting the number of Welt's deficiencies.

'You weren't serious about Pounder being polished off by his relatives? For the money?'

'Certainly not. Simply endeavouring to take that policeman's attention off the community living in the cathedral close.' Dean Hitt shook his head. 'Ewart Jones's fault, you see. For making himself so vulnerable. Spoiling the clerical mystique. Clive Brastow was right about that. In a way. Wouldn't do to tell him so,' he added frowning. 'But Ewart's frolics really have made us all look too fallible.'

'They were intended in what you'd term a good cause.' Treasure's now practised defence of the Precentor worked in an almost reflex way.

'Accepted. But he wasn't the only one ready to adopt stern measures. Or to have his acts mirror his conviction, for that matter. Tell you something in strictest confidence to indicate how much people care.' The Dean took a draught of sherry, smacking his lips before tabling the actual revelation. 'So far as I know, Nutkin is only moderately rich, but he's certainly our biggest single recent benefactor. Donated fifty thousand pounds to the Fabric Fund a few years ago. Anonymously. I knew, but nobody else does. It covered the cost of some absolutely vital work. You won't mention that to anyone?'

'Of course not.'

'Illustrates my point, don't you think?'

'What point, darling?' asked Margaret Hitt, who had just entered the room. 'Don't get up, either of you. What's the latest news of Ursula?' she continued, without waiting for an answer to the first question.

'Condition satisfactory,' the Dean replied.

'Good.' She eyed the two glasses. 'You've not forgotten we're all overdue at the Merits' sherry party?'

'I don't believe I am,' said Treasure.

'Yes, you are. We were deputed to invite you, but Gilbert's obviously forgotten.'

'Quite right. Sorry, Treasure. Knew there was something. You'll come, won't you?'

'Delighted.'

'You won't be really,' put in Mrs Hitt. 'But it'll certainly delight Algy and the others to have an eminent outsider present. Mr Pounder's death and Ursula's antic will have shed a blight on the proceedings, of course. What exactly did she say in that letter to you?'

Treasure told her, adding: 'The Chief Inspector seemed less concerned about the letter than he did about her having pheno-barbitone handy.'

'Ursula couldn't have laced Mr Pounder's tea, if that's what he's thinking. Nor done anything else to him,' said the Dean's wife firmly. 'Much too timid.'

'I really believe she regarded writing to me as much worse than just a mistake. I also blame myself for telling her this morning I'd intended voting for the sale.'

'Making her feel spurned, you think?' Mrs Hitt questioned without conviction.

'Or worse. An embarrassment to her husband perhaps,' offered the banker.

Mrs Hitt frowned at him. 'So that she needed to take the blame?'

'Or advertise her guilt?'

'Or cover his?' the Dean put in. 'I mean his shortcomings generally. As a husband. At least, I think that's what I mean.'

'Glad you could come.' Canon Algy Merit greeted Treasure, steering him further into the crowded drawing room at the Chancellor's house. 'Unfortunate day for a party, as it's turned out. But it is my birthday. And we can't alter that.'

Justification was implicit not only in the words but also in the benign gaze the Canon spread over the assembled company. He was affirming that, unpredicted murders and suicide attempts notwithstanding, birthdays were feasts of obligation observed for the very reason that they were predicted. His stout person was positively shining in the silk cassock and cape, as were his cheeks and the dome of his head. Only what was left of the curly hair, plastered down for the occasion, exposed a recalcitrant element. It had become decidedly springy at the sides.

The room was grand and elegant and immediately impressed with its double walnut doors in a pedimented casing and its original fretted friezes. What the visitor could see of the furnishings he found equally to his taste. The colours of the walls and drapes were fresh and new, but well fitting to the period of the house.

'What a gorgeous room.'

'Good of you to approve,' said Olive Merit, who was now standing before Treasure holding a small silver tray with some filled glasses on it. 'Dry or medium sherry?'

He helped himself to a glass of the paler liquid. 'Not difficult to see highly creative minds have been at work on the decorations,' he offered tactfully, not knowing which of the Merits might have been responsible.

'It helps to have the basics designed or at least inspired by Christopher Wren,' the Canon replied, the satisfaction in the tone suggesting the further inspiration had been provided by himself.

'Hasn't helped much next door,' said his sister flatly. 'One regrets the Brastows have quite lost the sense of style in the Treasurer's House. They practically live in the kitchen. Give the rest over to good works, garish posters and trestle tables. Poor Ursula. She really made an effort converting the basement into a flat for fugitives, but once people see it they seem to prefer staying on the run.'

'Let me introduce you to someone you haven't met,' put in Merit. 'The Lord Lieutenant of the County isn't here yet,' he added airily, as though that luminary had delayed an earlier appearance for reasons any member of the *cognoscenti* would perfectly understand.

'Surprisingly, there aren't many here I don't know,' smiled Treasure, looking about the room. 'I'm sure I can look after myself.'

He could see the liberated Canon Jones talking earnestly with Miles Nutkin and Laura Purse. On the edge of the same group Glynis Jones, who waved to him, was standing with Gerard Twist and Mrs Nutkin, who Treasure had been introduced to on the doorstep as he was arriving. The Dean and his wife, who he had come with, had quickly been buttonholed by the woman standing beside Bliter and who Treasure guessed would be Mrs Bliter. It was this quartet the banker joined.

'Mr Treasure, don't believe you've met Jennifer Bliter,' Mrs Hitt offered, without wasting much time on formal introductions. 'Commander Bliter has been telling us the head verger's just been found drowned. In the river. It's quite a shock. I was speaking to him at five-thirty.' The normally serene woman was clearly disconcerted by the news.

'I was going to ask, was he . . . er . . . ?' Bliter punctuated with a cough. Was he quite himself then?'

'What Percy means is was he blotto?' put in Mrs Bliter with a slight slur suggesting she wasn't entirely sober herself. 'I mean they're obviously going to think he fell over the bridge drunk.'

'He smelled of peppermint,' said Mrs Hitt.

'He usually did,' her husband commented. 'You say he went in over the bridge?'

'One of the bridges, the police think,' Bliter affirmed. 'Probably the old.' He turned to Treasure. 'It's not that uncommon, I'm afraid. Dangerously low parapet for the unwary. They rang me to find out what time he went off duty. I didn't know for sure.' He looked at his watch. 'I shall have to leave shortly, to see his family. In case there's anything we can do.'

'Good of you,' muttered the Dean.

'I think he was all right when we spoke,' Mrs Hitt said, and now in a normal firm voice. She glanced at Treasure, who she'd told earlier about her exchange with Duggan. 'I suppose there'll be an examination. Perhaps he had a giddy spell?' There was a momentary embarrassed silence.

'If he was crossing the river, he wasn't on his normal route home,' Bliter broke in.

'It's almost as though there's a curse on Litchester vergers,' said Laura Purse gravely. She had just appeared beside Treasure. 'Very sad for his wife. Come and circulate,' she added, putting an arm through his and leading him away after exchanging nods with Mrs Hitt 'We have to share out important strangers in our closed society. Everyone's expected to avoid the subject of Mrs Brastow, but Duggan hardly makes for light relief.'

He smiled. 'Has Glynis mentioned the Daras family still exists and is . . . ?'

'Busy terrorising Much Stratton?' Laura completed. 'Yes, she just told me. Daras himself sounds pretty awful.'

'Daras? Isn't that the family . . . ?' began Mrs Nutkin, who was just within hearing.

'They started out as d'Aras. Old Border County family. Came over with the Conqueror. Good evening, Mr Treasure.' This was Nutkin, who had turned about to speak.

'Means they've been here nearly as long as you, dear,' added Mrs Nutkin with a deep chuckle. She was a jolly woman, a little dumpy, but loosely elegant, and younger than her husband. 'Weren't they clients of your grandfather's, Miles?'

'Probably. I gather you've been to see them?' Nutkin asked.

'Put on to them by someone who assumed I'd be interested in a Magna Carta copy, and probably knew Daras might have one,' the banker answered.

'As well as some quite unmentionable habits,' Glynis Jones observed loudly from the far side of a widening circle.

'Did they show you a copy?' asked Mrs Nutkin.

'No. But Daras himself suggested the local seventeenth-century ones were impossible to tell from the real thing.'

'Might be difficult, certainly,' offered Laura slowly.

'In which case it's been pointless using the expensive kind. Could we get a couple on the cheap? One to sell, and another for the cathedral? To replace the old one?' Amused, most people turned towards the speaker, Gerard Twist, who reddened slightly at his own boldness.

'Good idea. Who'd care anyway?' agreed Mrs Nutkin jovially.

'Almost anyone who'd been conned into paying over a million pounds for a copy,' declared Canon Jones.

'More sherry?' Olive Merit was at Treasure's side, holding a decanter. 'And does one gather you've been acting the detective on our behalf today?'

'No, one doesn't,' the banker replied, although it so happened the answers to a number of vexing questions had just become plain to him. 'Of course, I've been given charge of an invaluable relic which, with the Dean and Chapter's permission, I propose to have properly examined and dated.'

'You mean that lump of wax?' This was Canon Jones again. 'The wax from the seal on our Magna Carta?'

'That's right. I'm advised by an expert it contains enough carbon to allow for accurate dating.'

'So at least it will re-authenticate our dear but destroyed exemplification of 1225,' said Laura.

'How exciting,' enthused Mrs Nutkin. 'Do you have the wax with you?'

'Sorry, no. It's in my room at the Red Dragon. I suppose I should have . . .'

Treasure's words were drowned by the noisy verbal explosions at the door. A thoroughly dishevelled Welt was standing there in what seemed to be a very drunken condition. 'Evening, all. Evening, comrades. Come to say happy birthday to Algy. Where's Algy?' he called, swaying on the threshold. 'Here to prove my innocence as well. Not invited. Still, thought you'd like to know I'm up to no harm.' He roughly pushed away a male guest. 'Not staying. Don't worry. Thought you ought to know I haven't ab . . . ducted Miss Larks. Only been thrown out of the lounge bar of the Bridge Hotel for being pi . . . sozzled, begging the ladies' pardons.' He looked about him, waving a hand as a further general greeting and rocking on his heels. 'Saw one of the honoured guests at this . . . at this august assembly crossing the bridge. Very su . . . su . . . superior. Didn't deign to see me. Didn't want to know someone being asked to leave the . . . the lounge bar of the Bridge Hotel. Just as well. No condition to be ack . . . nowledged. Had a little snooze since then. But haven't ab . . . ab . . . ki . . . dnapped Cindy. She's just been run out of town, or out of her tiny mind, by Christian gossip. Frightened out of her wits. By charitable and loving kindness. Like Ursula Brastow and a few others who haven't survived this hothouse. Like that poor bloody outsider Welt, is what you'll be saying next week.'

'Disgusting!'

'I think so, too, Mrs Commander Bliter. Or should it be Commander of the Bliters? Captain of the Snoopers? Ay, ay, Mrs Commander. Don't worry, I've been to the cops. When I worked out you'd fingered me. So I've owned up. Nothing left on your conscience.'

After exchanging nods, Treasure and Gerard Twist had begun threading through the guests towards Welt.

'Well, Happy Christmas to all. Thank you for having me. And, before the heavies get to me, may you all rot in hell.' Roaring out the last words, Welt swung around, swayed and would have fallen if he hadn't managed to throw his arms around the neck of the Lord Lieutenant, who an astonished Algy Merit was just ushering into the room.

# Chapter Eighteen

'Dr Welt got in because Canon Merit had left the front door open. He was showing the Lord Lieutenant where to park his car,' giggled Glynis Jones, waiting with Laura Purse and Gerard Twist in the busy front hall of the Red Dragon. 'It really was an outstanding performance.'

'Well, Olive didn't think so. I thought she was going to bring the salver down on his head,' said Laura. 'She was beside herself with fury.'

'And not without cause,' agreed Treasure, who had now rejoined them. 'I've fixed the table and ordered our food, so if nobody wants a drink I suggest we go in.' He had invited the three to dine with him. He had extended the invitation to others at the Merits' party but all of them had already made dinner arrangements, some at this hotel. 'I see the Nutkins are in the bar with Mrs Bliter,' he added.

'I spoke to them as they came in,' said Twist. 'They're waiting dinner till the Commander gets back from seeing the Duggan family.'

'Funny, I thought I saw him just now,' offered Glynis to Treasure as they trailed the others into the restaurant. The banker glanced at the pigeon-holes beside the reception desk as they passed. He had done the same earlier.

The head waiter guided the group across to the table Treasure had requested. From the seat he was taking the banker had a clear view through the open doorway to the single lift entrance in the hall, as well as the stairs beside it. 'Sorry your parents couldn't join us,' he said to Glynis as he held out her chair.

'Mummy's not back yet. Dad said they both might join us for coffee later. If that's all right. He's got an extra sermon to get ready for the weekend.'

'And wasted the time he should have spent writing it in the police station. He told me,' said Laura, smiling. 'He really is very conscientious. I wouldn't miss a good dinner to write a sermon.'

'It's more than that actually,' Glynis offered. 'Accumulation of business. And his tummy's upset.'

'There's Mrs Hitt with Canon Brastow.' Laura nodded towards the door, and following Treasure's interested gaze.

'Good of the Hitts to take Brastow under their wing tonight,' said the banker. 'I suggested they join us if they found him in, but they thought he'd probably rather avoid company. I'm surprised they got him to come here. Hope he lasts the course.'

'Wonder what's happened to the Dean?' remarked Twist, head turned to see what was going on.

'Somewhere about on his own,' said Glynis. 'He likes coming here because he knows the layout so well. With his white stick he moves round the place like a sighted person. As he does in the cathedral. And the close.'

'The more time I spend with your Dean, the less conscious I become of his single disability, and the more aware I am that mine are legion.'

'He has that effect on most thinking people, Mr Treasure,' Laura acknowledged. 'He's immensely well informed. Did you notice he knew more about carbon dating than I did? Bit deflating for an antiquarian.'

'Not for me, though. I never heard of it till tonight,' admitted Glynis.

'Principle's quite simple,' said Treasure. 'Most substances can be dated through analysis of their carbon element. Beeswax is one of them.'

'Fancy your knowing that.'

'I didn't, Glynis. Not for sure. But when we got back this afternoon I rang a friend. An industrial chemist. He said my bit of wax could probably be dated within a hundred years. Good enough, one would think, to establish if it had been the seal on a thirteenth-century document.'

'Proving the Litchester Magna Carta couldn't have been a fake?' asked Twist.

'It was genuine all right,' said Laura with spirit.

'Though you weren't sure how scientific the authentication was four years ago. And before that whether the thing had just been accepted as genuine because it had been around a long time,' Treasure observed.

'With plenty of evidence about its location through the centuries,' rejoined the librarian. 'Unlike the Salisbury Cathedral Magna Carta. That disappeared without trace for a whole century before turning up again in 1814.'

'But there's nothing to prove the Litchester copy couldn't have been swapped at any point? For instance, the Dean told me there's a story one of your predecessors used to take it home for safe-keeping every night. Hid it under her bed because she was convinced the current Dean was planning to sell it without telling anyone.'

Laura nodded with a wan smile. 'True, I'm afraid. That was before the last war. When our librarian was unpaid. I'm told she was a maiden lady of impeccable virtue if no great physical attraction. Her bed was probably the safest place in England.'

'Hm. But carrying the thing backwards and forwards must have had its hazards. It just illustrates . . .' Treasure, whose gaze had strayed to the door again, nodded a greeting to a couple who had just entered. 'Isn't that the cathedral architect and his wife? They were at the Merits', too.'

'That's right. The Smithson-Bows,' said Glynis, breaking up a bread stick. 'You probably think this restaurant is a sort of cathedral annexe.'

'The party certainly seems to have moved on here. Almost *en masse*. Except for the Merits themselves.'

'They'll still be coping with hangers-on,' Twist put in. 'The cathedral hierarchy get a discount from the Red Dragon management. Arranged by the Commander. Friday night we tend to take advantage of it. If at all. It's still pretty pricey.' He looked up in surprise at the head waiter, who had appeared at his side.

'Telephone call for you, Mr Twist. In the box on the right in the hall, sir.'

'Thank you.' Twist seemed embarrassed. 'Sorry. Shan't be a moment.' He got up and hurried out.

'It's a pity the discount Gerard was talking about doesn't apply to our visitors, even very important ones,' remarked Glynis seriously.

'Never mind. I expect we'll get out without having to do the washing-up,' joked Treasure. He tried the Chablis the wine waiter had just poured for him to taste. 'Good. Very good.' He looked up at the man and nodded. 'This should see us through the smoked salmon when it comes. Meantime would both you ladies excuse me for a minute? Something important I've forgotten in my room. Do drink up. There's another bottle cooling.'

He crossed the room, acknowledging a wave from Mrs Hitt. Instead of going straight to the lift, he crossed the hall. Mrs Nutkin and Mrs Bliter were still at a table in the bar as he passed. He didn't need to go right up to the reception desk to see his key was missing, nor did he ask the porter if he knew who had taken it. The telephone box was empty.

There was no one else waiting for the lift, which was already on its way down. It arrived almost as soon as Treasure pressed the button. The doors slid open to reveal Len Hawker standing alone inside looking miserable and clutching a hotel key. He made to get out but the banker pushed him back, pressing the button and barring his way until the doors shut again and they were on their way up to the third floor.

'That key, please,' ordered Treasure, holding out his hand.

'This one? It's mine.' But the other handed it over nervously all the same. 'You've heard about the verger? Duggan? I spoke to him this morning. In the cathedral. It was his son put me on to Much Stratton. I'm going to the police. I don't want to be mixed up in any of this. Not any more. I'm . . .'

The doors opened at the third floor. Treasure thrust the key back at Hawker. It was the key to room 216. 'You're very wise. The police will want to know the name of your client. If I were you, I'd tell them. And I'd go right now.'

He pressed the ground-floor button and stepped out of the lift, watching the doors close on the bewildered private investigator, who was winking without cease. He turned the corner into the carpeted corridor, trying but failing to stop his footsteps reverberating through the old timber joists. There were eight bedrooms on the left-hand side facing on to the courtyard at the rear of the building. His room, number 320, was at the end. He could see the key hanging in the lock. He didn't stop outside the room but went past it through a swing door labelled FIRE PROTECTION.

The Dean was standing to the left on the other side of the door. His back was half-turned away from Treasure. He was pressing against the release bar of the door to the outside fire escape. Now he spun about sharply, grasping his folded white stick in a clenched fist.

'It's Treasure.'

'Well, that's a blessing,' whispered the Dean in a relieved voice. 'We were right?'

'I think so. From the sound of the walk. Went into your room a minute ago. Don't believe he'll be leaving this way. Bar's stuck. Can't try shifting it without making a racket. Told you this place was a comfortable death-trap.'

'Leave it. Just stay against the wall through here.'

The two went back to the main corridor. Treasure pressed his ear to the door and listened. He could hear sounds of movement inside the room – of cupboards and drawers being opened and shut.

Taking hold of the key, he turned it in the lock. The door didn't move. 'Bolted on the inside,' he said over his shoulder. He rapped on the door, shouting 'Open up,' and rapped again, adding: 'This is Mark Treasure. You won't find what you're looking for. Just open the door, please.'

The noises stopped abruptly. Then came the sound of someone

moving quickly through the room. Something was overturned, then came a hammering, followed by the distinctive screech of a window being thrown up.

'Not possible,' said Treasure. 'It must be a forty-foot drop.'

'Is the fire escape within reach of the window?' asked the Dean.

'No. I looked earlier. No ledge, either. You could try jumping, but I don't think I would.'

'You might if you were desperate,' cautioned the Dean, pushing back through the swing door. 'We've got to get this door open.'

'Let me.' Treasure lifted a foot and began jabbing it at the bar: the door sprang open at the third attempt. The cold air smote him as he rushed out on to the metal platform, but what he saw froze him in a different way. 'Don't. You won't make it,' he cried – but he was too late. The unathletic figure was already in the air.

The grip of the outstretched fingers destined for the staircase railing was never tested. The awkward sideways leap had lacked the needful thrust to match its boldness. The reach was shortened in a move of despair, it seemed, even before its aim was certain of missing. Inanely the hands had been drawing back to protect the terrified, well-fed face – a face fixed with the look of terror that was to stay in Treasure's mind. There was no scream, but a second later the body hit the top of a parked car with a sickening thud.

'It was the Dean who knew you were here,' said Treasure. 'He even borrowed a key from Canon Brastow.'

'He didn't say I'd broken in?' Cowering in a big old armchair in the Brastows' empty basement flat, Cindy Larks for once looked younger than her age, very frightened, and a good deal less alluring than the last time Treasure had seen her. In this dishevelled state she also bore a remarkable resemblance to two other young women he'd become acquainted with during the day. Her arms were clasped around her body. It was cold in the room. 'I came in when they was all fussing over Mrs Brastow, you know? When the ambulance was outside? I didn't mean no harm. It was just somewhere to come. To hide.' She looked appealingly from Treasure to Olive Merit, who was also seated opposite her.

'What did you intend doing next?'

'Don't know really. Except I been waiting so I could see a friend.'

'Dr Welt?' Miss Merit put in quietly.

'That's right, miss.'

'You had an arrangement to see him at seven-fifteen?'

The girl's face took on a cunning expression. 'Couldn't go then in case the police knew. In case they was waiting.'

'*Were* waiting. You could have come to me in the first place, Cindy.'

'Didn't like to, miss. Not in case I got you in trouble, you know?'

'I gather you're related to the Daras family?'

She nodded in answer to Treasure's question. 'Miss Merit knows. Old Mr Daras is my grandpa. Only I couldn't go there. He chucked my mother out years ago. And he could have known about me and Mr Pounder. He'd taken against Mr Pounder, too.'

'D'you want to tell us about you and Mr Pounder?'

'That I killed him? Is that what you want me to say? Well, I did, see? I didn't mean to. And I didn't know about the money then. Not about him leaving me money.'

'Tell us about your relationship with him, Cindy. Were you his mistress?'

'I didn't go to bed with him, miss. Nothing like that. He paid me.'

'To do what?'

The girl swallowed, glancing at Treasure. 'To lie on the table. Every Thursday in the Old Library. For quarter of an hour. After ten past six.'

'That was all?'

'No, miss.' She had lowered her voice and her gaze. 'I had to . . . to lift my skirt, like, and . . . He never touched me. Just looked at me. And held my scarf. Or my hanky. Up to his chest.'

'But he talked to you?'

'Sometimes. Not always.'

'And he paid you for that?'

'Twenty pounds. Cash. Kinky really. Didn't ever fancy doing anything else with him, though. Wouldn't have, I don't think. He was so old. And last night, when he went mad . . .'

'How d'you mean – *mad*?' This was Treasure.

'Real mad. Like someone crazy. Something upset him. About selling the Magna Carta. At first he was talking to himself. Not taking no notice . . . any notice of me. Kept going on about people being too greedy. Not having values or something. Spoiling things for other people. It didn't make sense, you know? And he was getting redder in the face all the time.'

'You didn't say anything?'

'In the end I said you had to make allowances like, and he jumped up and stood over me all angry. Said I was like the rest. Ungrateful. Then he went to strangle me. God's honour. He wasn't being sexy or anything like that. Just violent. He was strong, though. I thought he was going to kill me. That's when I hit him.'

'You hit him with the mace?'

'No, with my fists. We were struggling, and when he fell the mace came down on top of him. Off the table behind me. I wasn't meaning to kill him. Just wanted to get away. He kind of slipped under the table the first time. Then when he tried getting up the mace fell on him. I thought he was getting up again. I just rolled off the table and ran.'

'You pulled the door behind you?'

'Yes.'

'And locked it, taking the key with you?' Miss Merit pressed.

'Yes. I thought it'd stop him coming after me. By that door. Except he couldn't have, could he? He died when the mace hit him, didn't he?' She sunk her head in her hands. 'Oh God, and I didn't care. Not then. Not till today. I was numb, see? Then when I heard about the money.' She let out a sob. 'He meant well. Lost his temper the once, that was all.'

'Is that why you ran away today? Because you were ashamed?'

'Not exactly, miss. It was the money. The police know I killed him. I had the motive, see? Like on the telly. Except I didn't know about it.'

Miss Merit looked appealingly at Treasure, who gave a negative shake of his head.

'You didn't cry "Rape" or anything when you were getting away? When you got down the stairs?' he asked.

'Why should I? He didn't try to rape me. I didn't want people knowing what I'd been doing. For money. If it all came out. People wouldn't have believed it was just . . . well, you know.'

'I think so. Tell me – the paraffin heater in the library, was it between you and Mr Pounder?'

The girl looked up. 'No. Behind him.'

'And he fell..?'

'Under the table, like I said.'

'That's where his body was found, Cindy. How d'you suppose he tipped the fire over?'

'He couldn't have. It was too far away.'

'So how d'you suppose the fire started?'

'The heater must have been leaking. It was old.'

'It was doing that all right. It had been tipped over and the reservoir cover had come off. It may have been purposely unscrewed. Did you do that?'

''Course not.'

'Well, if Pounder died where you left him, he couldn't have, either.'

'Does it make any difference?'

'Quite a bit.' Treasure nodded at Miss Merit.

'Cindy, Mr Pounder died of asphyxia. Breathing in smoke. He wasn't dead when you left him. Stunned probably. Somebody else caused his death. The person who started the fire and left him there. A person with a much better motive than yours.' She waited a moment before continuing. 'Any idea who we've been talking about?'

The girl had burst into tears while Miss Merit was speaking. Now she dried her eyes and swallowed. The relief on her face was evident. When she began speaking her expression seemed guileless enough, but because it again recollected the family resemblance Treasure couldn't help steeling himself to allow for Daras natural duplicity.

'There's nobody I can think of,' she said, tight-lipped. And for the first time the innocence didn't wholly satisfy.

'You didn't see anyone? Anyone you haven't admitted seeing already?'

There was hesitation before she uttered, 'Nobody,' and shook her head.

'Dr Welt . . .'

'Oh, no,' she gasped. 'Not Donald, he couldn't. He wouldn't. Not for me, he wouldn't. He didn't stay. He just went in through the door and came back out again. Straight away. I don't know why.' And here was a blurted outcry that came straight from the heart, with no pretences.

'The Old Library door?'

'No. He never went near the library. The cloister door. I saw him. When I was waiting. He didn't see me. I was hiding like. In the cloister garden. Till Mr Pounder come out . . . Came out.'

'You were still hiding? Because you didn't want to explain to anyone what you'd been doing? Not even Dr Welt? You're sure of that?' Olive Merit sounded unconvinced.

'That's right, miss. But I wanted to see Mr Pounder when he was leaving. To say there was no hard feelings. About losing his temper, you know?'

'And perhaps to collect the twenty pounds he owed you?'

'That as well, miss. I suppose.' She looked down at the handkerchief she'd been kneading in her lap. 'But he never come out . . . Came out.'

'Did you not think you should go back and see he was all right?' asked Treasure.

'Not at first, I didn't. Then I thought he must have left by the other door.'

'You didn't think he might be lying up there hurt?'

'Not really.' This was whispered. 'Except . . .'

'Except what, Cindy?'

'Well, when I was thinking perhaps I ought to go back, Canon Jones went in.'

'That would be at about ten past seven,' Treasure said.

'About. And then I saw Don . . . Dr Welt coming back. So I went to wait for him at his front door. He thought I'd just got there.'

'And have you seen or spoken with Dr Welt today?'

'No, miss. Honest.'

'Well, you've just corroborated something he said about himself,' Treasure confirmed. 'A moment ago I was merely going to say the police believe he may be able to help them in pointing to someone else who could have been involved in Mr Pounder's death. Someone who died in an accident earlier tonight.'

The girl looked up. 'Not Canon Jones, was it? Like the police thought?'

Treasure glanced at Olive Merit. 'No, not Canon Jones. I'm afraid it was Mr Nutkin, the Chapter Clerk.'

# Chapter Nineteen

'I'm sure Miss Merit being there loosened the girl's tongue,' said Treasure. 'Astute of you to know where Cindy had been all day. And that she'd been mixed up in Pounder's demise.'

The Dean smiled pensively. 'Just . . . just following my nose.'

'You'd have obliged by telling us a bit earlier, sir,' said Detective Chief Inspector Pride reflectively but without rancour. He stirred his coffee.

'I considered it, Mr Pride. But there seemed no purpose in leading you to suspect a probably innocent girl. You might have arrested her and slacked off finding the real culprit. Temporarily, of course,' the cleric added, but with only the degree of tempering he considered appropriate. He was getting his own back for what he considered the police mishandling of Canon Jones.

It was eleven o'clock on Saturday morning. The three men were seated in Dean Hitt's study. Mrs Hitt had provided coffee then left, she said, to complete an important errand. She and Treasure had talked briefly alone when she had let him in.

'The girl was very nearly culpable, sir,' said the policeman, then immediately wishing he hadn't. He hoped the others would overlook the observation.

'Difficult that,' mused Treasure promptly. 'Like being a tiny bit pregnant.' He glanced mischievously at the policeman, then turned to their host. 'Dean, why don't you tell Mr Pride just how you knew about Cindy's relationship with Pounder?'

The Dean sniffed. 'He was a creature of habit. Or his laundress was. Probably his daughter. He changed his shirt once a week. On Sundays. For more than a year on Fridays he's always reeked of a loathsome but distinctive cheap scent which stayed on him till Saturdays. Same thing recurred every week. Seemed to me he picked it up from Cindy Larks. She's the only female in the community I know who wears the stuff. Fairly assaults you when she even passes. She passes me. Often twice a day. When the choir leaves the chancel after services. As I say, Pounder used to acquire the smell between evensong on Thursdays and matins on Fridays. Since he slept at his daughter's and Cindy Larks spends her late Thursday evenings with Donald Welt, it didn't require a massive intellect to know when he got the stuff on him – and roughly how.' He stopped himself from adding that Welt also had the same scent about him from time to time.

'Curiously, your wife says she doesn't find the scent at all intrusive,' said Treasure. 'For instance, she didn't notice it at the Brastows' when you called for the Canon last night. I must say, I wasn't conscious of it when I went there, either.'

'Well, I found it impossible to ignore.'

'Depends on how well a person's olfactory sense is developed,' observed Pride learnedly, and to the mild surprise of the others.

The Dean nodded. 'Agreed in principle, but in this case it also had to do with a probably idiosyncratic distaste for the stuff. After all, it must be sold on a commercial basis. If most people dislike it as much as I do, the makers would go bust.'

'In any event, it explains why you were so certain Cindy was in that basement flat,' said Treasure.

'Quite certain,' said the Dean emphatically.

'You were right about the girl's grandfather having no time for her, Mr Treasure. Almost the first thing he admitted when I got out there last night.'

'Before the more substantial confessions. He'd gone off Pounder, too, you say, despite their having been army buddies?'

'In a way, yes, sir. Seems that's why Pounder left money to the girl. Sort of compensation for her grandfather being mean to her.'

'And his own conscience, I expect.' This was Treasure. 'Even so, I assume it was Daras money. Or, rather, money given to Daras by Nutkin for passing on.'

'That's the gist of it, sir. Like you predicted, Nutkin bought a Magna Carta copy from Daras three years ago. It's reasonable to suppose Nutkin substituted it for the original, which he then sold to a dishonest collector.'

'Reasonable but unproven,' Treasure put in heavily. 'With the added supposition that the buyer of whatever was sold was the unknown American bidder of three years ago. And the same party who sent Hawker here on Thursday.'

'I should think so, sir. And we got a name from Hawker, when he was running scared last night. It's another private investigator, of course. In Miami, Florida. Unlikely to divulge the name of *his* client, probably, but there's time enough for that.'

'And nobody noticed the switch?' put in the Dean.

'If there was one,' said Treasure, staring hard at the police-man. 'According to Laura Purse, a seventeenth-century facsimile produced in the scriptorium here could have been pretty well indistinguishable from the original. It might not have withstood a special expert scrutiny, but there's been no occasion for one of those from the likely time of any substitution until this week. Only Pounder twigged what might have happened.'

'Even though he wasn't an expert,' said Pride.

Immediately the Dean commented: 'Not an expert in the tech-nical sense. But he cared more about that parchment than he did for most things. Knew enough to spot it if something was wrong. Or even sense it.'

'But not report it, sir?'

'To have gone to what he knew had to be the source of any substitution. His friend Daras,' argued Treasure. 'Is that right, Mr Pride?'

'Who bribed him into keeping his mouth shut. That's correct, sir.'

The Dean made a face at the policeman's words. 'I trust some kind of finesse had to be applied.'

'It did, sir. Daras isn't admitting it directly, but he's implied Pounder accepted the switch was official but had to be kept dark. That the proceeds were going towards maintaining the cathedral.'

'And he believed it,' said the Dean, sighing. 'Even stopped referring to knowing about a source of Magna Carta copies. Of course, he was really a very simple man. And there was one large anonymous donation to the Fabric Fund at the time. What you might call Nutkin's conscience money, because that's what it was. That and the hope I'd add it to his catalogue of good works when the Chapter came to recommend him for inclusion in the Honours List. Pounder would have known about the donation – everybody did – but not who had made it.'

'A simple man with a venal side, sir.'

'You mean he was easily talked into taking his share?' This was Treasure.

'About taking half of what Daras told him he got for the copy, sir. That's what Daras said last night.'

'As straightforward as that? He wasn't told who'd done the buying?'

'No, sir. And, as you said, the money didn't really come from Daras. Only through him. And it wasn't part of his takings. It was an extra thirty-five thousand provided by Nutkin. Stuck in Daras's throat, that did. He figured if Nutkin could afford a fat sweetener for Pounder, then he, Daras should have got more in the first place. Seems it's what soured his relations with Pounder later.'

'I wonder how much Nutkin did get?' Treasure mused. 'Four hundred thousand, perhaps? Less the hundred and twenty thousand for Daras, Pounder, and what he gave to the cathedral. He probably cleared well over a quarter of a million.'

'And Daras volunteered all you've told us, Mr Pride?' the Dean asked doubtfully.

'Pretty well, sir. When he knew Nutkin was dead, and I faced him with the fact he stood to be accused as an accessory to Pounders' murder.'

'That was a bit sharp.'

'You should ask Mr Treasure about that, sir. It was his idea.'

The Dean grunted. 'Mightn't Nutkin have sold the copy and left our Magna Carta where it was?'

'Highly possible,' said Treasure vehemently and with a conviction he didn't feel nearly as strongly as the emphasis suggested. 'Something we'll never know for sure, of course.' He paused to allow Pride to weigh the point. 'One has to admit a substitution seems the more likely event. In the circumstances.' He paused again, firmly to demonstrate his objectivity.

'Except our own expert, Miss Purse, didn't spot it,' put in the Dean.

'Right. It was only the amateur Pounder who, it seems, may have smelled a rat,' agreed Treasure. The policeman simply looked thoughtful as the banker went on. 'Of course, a crooked buyer would almost certainly have his purchase authenticated, whereas the Magna Carta on show here would go on being accepted as it had been for centuries. And Nutkin must have been sure that in turning down an offer for four hundred thousand pounds the Chapter was effectively saying it had no intention of selling the Magna Carta. Not ever.'

'And that it would never need to have it validated. He was wrong on both counts, of course.' The Dean fingered the saucer of his coffee-cup. 'And you became convinced last evening, when we were at the Merits', that Nutkin was the villain?'

'For three slim and unrelated reasons that fuse into a big one when you think about them,' Treasure explained. 'Nutkin had almost certainly known the Daras family since his youth. He was the only person I'd told I'd changed my mind about selling, and he just as certainly carried barbiturates and hadn't admitted it. It was Glynis Jones who said to me yesterday that Daras must have had professional help – with his accounts, collecting rents and so on. Then Mrs Nutkin implied the Daras family had been clients of the Nutkin family firm for three generations. It was a reasonable guess that as a young articled clerk Nutkin had been the Darases' rent collector and general legal factotum.'

'He was, sir. And the firm still is. And it was how he came to know about the Magna Carta copy.'

Treasure nodded. 'After he'd talked to me on the telephone on Thursday afternoon, Nutkin had very little time for taking avoiding action. But he needed to take some. And pretty swiftly, for fear the Magna Carta was spirited away to the vault of a local bank. Remember, the potential buyers were a good deal more security conscious than the Chapter had been.'

'And they'd certainly have had the thing validated,' said the Dean slowly.

'And exposed as a fake, if it was. To which one could say "So what?"' the banker observed. 'Could a fraud have been traced to Nutkin?'

'Without doubt, sir. In time. He couldn't have risked it. Knowing Daras.'

The Dean cleared his throat. 'I prefer to believe he'd have seen exposure of a fake as something that would have cost the cathedral over a million pounds. That he'd have felt responsible for that loss, and that he saw a way of avoiding it. He was a strange chap with a strong conscience.'

The policeman threw Treasure a look redolent of disbelief but he said nothing.

'Was he especially religious?' asked the banker.

'I doubt it, though he may have thought he was. People can delude themselves in that area,' replied the Dean. 'Fact is, up to last Thursday he'd got away with a large haul of cash without actually harming anyone. And he'd given back a bit of it. Now it seems he was about to rob us of a much bigger sum. Morally indefensible? Condemning himself to everlasting damnation? Depends on how he saw it.'

'But then he committed a murder, sir.'

'Possibly unintentionally, you said, Mr Pride. Earlier, when my wife was here. In any case . . .'

'That's certainly my theory,' Treasure interrupted. 'For whatever reason, I believe he was determined to destroy that Magna Carta. He had very little time to plan, and very few aids. For instance, he had no access to a key to the Old Library nor to the Charter case.'

'Of course, Ewart Jones had taken the Chapter House spares,' the Dean agreed.

'He'd discovered those had gone after Chapter meeting. So he had to get in while Pounder was in charge. He took a chance by lacing the chap's tea with barbiturates. I gather he made the opportunity for that by coming into evensong after everyone else. I think he planned to go up to the library later when the old boy was asleep, break open the case, and take the contents.'

'Not kill Pounder? Not start a fire?'

'Difficult to be sure, Dean, but isn't it more likely he changed his plan when he found Pounder already looking very dead indeed? Collapsed from heart failure, or else bludgeoned by a thief, as we all thought later. The paraffin stove was providential in the circumstances. I doubt he knew it'd be there, but it adapted perfectly to his purpose. Destroying the Magna Carta was a lot safer than taking it away. He must have been quite sure the fire wouldn't spread, or perhaps he intended raising the alarm himself later.'

'And was he just as sure Pounder was dead, I wonder, sir?' Pride paused, then proceeded to answer his own question. 'Well, I'd be inclined to give the benefit of the doubt on that one, I suppose. It's often hard to find a pulse on the very elderly – especially if you're in a panic. Heard enough coroners say as much.'

'All of which seems to have left Nutkin with the perfect solution, and a still relatively clear conscience,' added Treasure.

'Except he went on to murder Duggan, sir.'

'After he'd learnt from you, Chief Inspector, that he'd killed Pounder after all. Would that have made the difference?'

'Yes, sir,' was the pragmatic response. 'Since he knew Duggan was going to start blackmailing him. Him and Nora Jakes, Pounder's daughter.'

'How did he know that?' asked the Dean, surprised.

'Daras told him. Duggan was out at the farm yesterday afternoon. Seems Hawker's enquiries about how to reach Daras set him thinking, that and the trouble Rory Duggan had reported seeing when he was out there earlier. Patrick Duggan had worked out whatever was leading people to Daras at this time could have something to do with Magna Carta copies. When he heard Pounder had left that money he was sure Daras and Pounder had been doing a deal with someone. He'd tied that in with Pounder's murder. And he'd seen Nutkin going into the cathedral at twenty-five minutes past six on Thursday evening.'

'But he hadn't told the police?'

'Would never have done that, sir. Making his own arrangements, you might say. Seems he'd told Commander Baer he thought he'd seen Nutkin that night. The Commander said he must have been mistaken.'

Treasure smiled grimly. 'Bliter mentioned it in turn to Nutkin, apparently, who said airily that Duggan had quite definitely been mistaken. Bliter accepted his word and said as much to Duggan, who pretended to agree he'd been wrong . . .'

'Bliter having given him Pounder's job as a sweetener? I don't much care for that,' said the Dean.

'But you made Bliter cancel the offer.'

'Certainly I did. I suppose that's why Duggan went back to the truth?'

'But still not to the police, sir. First, he was convinced if Pounder had got money, then Daras had got more – and for a Magna Carta copy. He said so to Daras, who made the mistake of pleading that Pounder had tricked him into parting with a copy for practically nothing.'

'Which was a lie?'

'It was, sir. Then Daras begged Duggan not to involve him, and swore the money he said Pounder had paid him had come from someone important in Litchester. Straight away Duggan said that someone had to be Nutkin and that wasn't all Nutkin had been up to. He was half-guessing probably, but he'd got Daras in a real panic and he gave the game away. Duggan left saying if Nutkin and Pounder had done so well, then Nutkin and Pounder's daughter could afford to push a bit of the proceeds his way for keeping quiet.'

'How did Daras alert Nutkin that there was trouble?' the Dean asked.

'Telephoned him, sir. Straight after Duggan left. There's a call-box on the road near the farm. Seems to be their only link with civilisation and progress.'

'So Nutkin decided he had to do something about Duggan. Murder him. Seems a bit extreme,' the Dean commented without emotion.

'Difficult to see what else he could do except wait to be blackmailed or arrested for murder.' This was Treasure. 'Duggan could fix him either way, with the petrified Daras obviously ready if necessary to squeal to save his own skin. Unfortunately for Nutkin, Dr Welt saw him on the bridge. Told everybody at the party he'd seen one of us there. Coy about saying which of us at the time.'

'Seemed he was wanting to imply it was one of the ladies following him, sir. Don't know why.'

'I think I do, Mr Pride, and it's not important,' murmured the Dean.

'I see,' replied the policeman without seeing at all. 'Anyway, he confirmed to me this morning it was Nutkin he saw. Would have come out in routine investigations even if Nutkin hadn't died. Leaving him something to explain. Along with other things.'

'Like the sodium phenobarbitone? Treasure, you haven't said how you got on to that,' questioned the Dean.

'Nutkin suffered from *petit mal*.'

'Mild form of epilepsy?'

'That's right. Produced general seizures usually lasting a few seconds. The sufferer loses consciousness but sometimes isn't aware he's had an attack. Nutkin had one when he was with me yesterday. At breakfast. Not a serious one, but I don't believe he knew it had happened. I have a cousin who gets similar episodes. He likes people to tell him after the event. I didn't tell Nutkin. I suppose because I didn't know him well enough. Thought it might embarrass him. The point is, my cousin carries phenobarb on him always. I believe all epileptics do as a precaution. It's the specific drug for the condition. It seems Nutkin was no exception.'

'So it seems, sir,' said Pride.

'Can you establish the barbiturate in Pounder's tea came from Nutkin?' the Dean asked.

'Fairly certainly, sir. The lab report had narrowed it down to two brands. Our checks yesterday showed neither had been dispensed by any pharmacist in this area. Not recently anyway. Had us foxed, that did. But it seems when Nutkin developed epilepsy two years ago he went to some trouble to avoid people knowing. That's not uncommon, they say. He didn't consult his own doctor about it. Went to someone in Harley Street. Got his prescriptions filled in London, too. His wife knew of course.' Pride looked at Treasure, then at the time. 'That's it, then,' he declared emphatically. 'If you'll both excuse me, I'd best be going. Got a lot to do. Mr Treasure understands the rest of the situation, sir. Thank you for the coffee. I can see myself out.'

The policeman hurried to the door, opened it, but hesitated with his hand on the knob. He turned about and gave the banker a blatantly conspiratorial nod, while producing a cigarette-pack from his pocket with his free hand. Then he left.

# Chapter Twenty

'What got into him? enquired the Dean after the policeman's pre-cipitate departure.

'Doesn't want to be pinned down on some past and future aspects of the business. Matters not yet touched on. Not before witnesses in the plural,' Treasure replied.

'I see. But he's confided in you?'

'He came to breakfast. Likes kedgeree.' The last comment was clearly offered as commendation, or perhaps even expiation, for the Detective Chief Inspector's known shortcomings.

'So, for instance, did he know who tipped you off about Daras in the first place?'

'The phone message at the hotel? Sorry, I worked that out for myself last night. It was Olive Merit. She owned up when I faced her with it, too. She's been sold from the start on my abilities as a sleuth, wanted to lay a scent, but didn't want to look silly. She suspected the truth when she heard the Magna Carta had been burnt. Knew the Daras family was a possible source of copies . . .'

'How did she know that?'

'Through Cindy Larks, who she taught and befriended at the school. Cindy is half-Daras of course. Her mother had told her about the Daras copy years ago. Didn't mean anything to Cindy, but she'd happened to mention it to Miss Merit.'

'Cindy won't be dragged into court over all this? Over Pound-er's death?'

'To the coroner's court, I'm afraid. After that it largely depends on the coroner's verdict. Pride and I both believe he'll bring in an open verdict on Pounder, and accidental death on Nutkin.'

'An open verdict on Pounder would mean . . .'

'Insufficient evidence to establish exactly how the fire was started.'

'Cindy didn't start it.'

'And almost as certainly Nutkin did. However, all the evidence is circumstantial.'

'He drugged Pounder's tea.'

'We assume so. But no one saw him do it.'

'Duggan saw him going into the cathedral.'

'But not actually going up to the Old Library. And Pride doesn't feel any case could survive on the deceased Duggan's hearsay testimony. In fact he thinks it very unlikely a case would have survived solely on Duggan's testimony in any circumstances.'

'And Duggan's death?'

'Welt admits he was drunk when he saw Nutkin coming off the bridge. He didn't note the time, and he certainly didn't see anything untoward happening. Almost everyone thinks Duggan was drunk and fell in the river by himself. It's pretty certain the autopsy will show he'd been drinking a good deal. Never a day when he didn't, apparently.'

The Dean considered for a moment. 'And where does Pride stand on Nutkin's death?'

'It was an accident all right, but how's it supposed to have happened?'

'He went to use my bathroom. To clean up before dinner. With my knowledge. He was a long time. You and I went up to check he was all right. The lock had stuck. Before I had the chance to stop him he'd jumped for the fire escape, missed his hold and fell to his death. He'd also had a few drinks, of course. Made him too bold. It's substantially true.'

The Dean winced. 'And better than the unembellished truth.'

'Because it avoids an unnecessary scandal, and more pain for his wife.'

'Poor woman. No children, fortunately.' The clergyman nodded his assent to the subterfuge. 'Two deaths and no compensation for the loss of our Magna Carta. Our fake Magna Carta. A parlous outcome in every way.' He shook his head.

'You're discounting the million pounds in insurance money.'

'You're not serious? What burnt was a copy, surely?'

'It may have been but the hard evidence doesn't suggest that. It'd be difficult for anyone to prove it was a fake – and that includes the unfortunate insurance company. No one can swear Nutkin switched those parchments. If he didn't switch them, it meant he'd passed off the fake as the original. That was to his dishonest collector, who we know was already suspicious about what was happening.'

'Because this fellow Hawker was sent to check?'

'Precisely. Because it was reported a highly respectable museum was bidding for the Litchester exemplification.'

'What could the crook collector do in the circumstances? I mean if the present bidder had gone through with the purchase, presumably after having his own validation tests done?'

'Anything from demanding his money back to having Nutkin roughed up – or worse. Possibly much worse.'

'You don't say?'

'Hawker told me the buyer might have been a rich American hoodlum. The sort of person who might not care to be crossed. It's only supposition, of course.'

'But one which must have occurred to Nutkin. So he was in trouble whatever he did?' The Dean pondered for a moment. 'Aren't we forgetting that piece of wax? The wax from the seal?'

'If it was from the seal. And if it wasn't an old bit re-used for sealing different documents at different times. Laura Purse says beeswax was always being recycled in that way, and adulterated in the process.' The banker rose and walked over to a window, which offered a ravishing view of the cathedral: old stones bathed in the mid-winter morning sunlight. 'In any case, I'm afraid the lump's disappeared. I really did leave it in my room yesterday before lunch. And I haven't seen it since. Of course it looked quite worthless. Anyway, it's gone.' He turned about to study his host's reaction. 'As I say, the possibility of it actually proving the age of the document was pretty fanciful. You see, I didn't advertise the caveats that chemist added to what he told me on the phone.'

'Because you were baiting a trap. And the bait was taken,' the Dean put in dourly, rubbing his forehead. 'So, what we know is that Daras sold Nutkin a Magna Carta copy. We don't know what he did with it, hearsay and possibility not being evidence.'

'Precisely. What passed as the arrangements for the Magna Carta's safe-keeping may produce some argument, but I think the onus there will be on the insurance company. Your policy document stipulates the Charter had to be under human supervision when it wasn't under lock and key. The stipulations should have been sterner, but it seems to me the cathedral authorities obeyed them. And did so to the letter. The company could challenge you over whether they were fulfilled in the spirit. But if they took it to law I think they'd lose – basically because they were too lax.'

'Because they didn't believe anyone would want to pinch the thing, any more than we did. You really think they'll have to pay? And that morally we'll have the right to accept the money?'

'Yes. On both counts.' The banker shrugged. 'And it's not a question of morality. Just business.'

'And you and Pride believe the coroner won't press for criminal charges over Pounder's death?'

'Pretty sure of it.'

The Dean gave a loud grunt of satisfaction. He was to do the same several months later when Treasure's opinion over the insurance payout proved to be substantially correct. That came after the launch of the Litchester Cathedral Appeal, which eventually raised very nearly the target of two million pounds. Canon Jones had taken charge of the appeal after Clive Brastow and his wife left for West Africa when Canon Brastow accepted an important appointment there.

Treasure and the Detective Chief Inspector were also right about the outcome of the inquest over Pounder's death.

The Banker was aware some of these legal consequences might not match the facts nearly so well as they did natural justice and sound expediency. But he had known also on that Saturday morning that he was in good company with these conclusions.

After leaving the Deanery, the Honourable Mrs Hitt had reached the Lady Chapel just after the start of the ten o'clock communion service. She hadn't joined the small congregation. The chapel was raised five steps above the ambulatory – the aisle that went around it at the extreme east end of the cathedral. Below the steps, in a quiet corner of the space behind the cathedral high altar, there were a few chairs set beside a circular iron pricket stand where worshippers who chose could light candles in memory of departed souls. There were no candles burning when she arrived but Mrs Hitt set one on a pricket spike and lit it. Then she sat in one of the raffia-seat chairs watching the candle burn.

She said a silent prayer for Miles Nutkin – poor, misguided Nutkin with his reckless, dishonest schemes that were doomed to fail because his deepest inborn trait was timidity. His end had perfectly illustrated the gap between his aims and his achievements.

There was no doubt in her mind that Nutkin had made the Magna Carta substitution, and none, either, that he had done it primarily for personal gain. She hadn't known as much when she'd come face to face with him in the cathedral close just before five-fifteen on Thursday afternoon. She had been on her way to give a lecture at the municipal museum in Bridge Street. He had been coming away from the Chapter House.

'My dear Miles, you look as if you've seen a ghost,' she exclaimed. 'The Chapter meeting must be over. Where are the others? Are you sure you're all right.'

'They've gone. To evensong. All of them. Your husband's idea. To . . . to heal any rifts.' His commentary had been delivered in a lustreless monotone. He hadn't replied to her last enquiry, but continued to look pained and abstracted.

'You've agreed to disagree?'

'The exemplification will be sold. I've just talked to Mark Treasure. On the telephone. He's changed his mind. Could you credit, the man has changed his mind?' He had seemed to over-balance.

'Miles, something is wrong with you.' She had taken his arm.

'I'm all right. All right,' he'd repeated as if to convince himself. 'It's simply hard to believe.'

Clearly he was taking it badly – losing out over a principle. 'You feel it's a betrayal?' She remembered looking back at the Old Library before quoting: 'But you shouldn't be *betrayed by what is false within*. You know the Magna Carta is a false . . .'

'I know no such thing!' he had nearly shouted.

At the time his reaction had been inexplicable. The quotation – from Meredith – had seemed apposite: they had made a false god out of an artefact which was now to be bartered. But Nutkin had roughly pushed away from her – dropping her arm after she had felt the shudder go through him: such a very electric response to the mildest of admonitions. And without another word he had turned on his heel and hurried away from her, back the way he had come.

That chance encounter had stayed in her mind. Soon after it had not been difficult to accede to a conviction that Nutkin had done something outrageous. And she was now sure he had died attempting to purloin the one piece of evidence he believed could condemn him.

Margaret Hitt had told no one of that meeting nor of her growing presentment. But her inner conviction had steeled her through the previous day not so much to see that justice took its course as to see injustice didn't.

'. . . *unto whom all hearts be open, all desires known, and from whom no secrets are hid* . . .' The voice of Canon Jones, celebrant at this extra saint's day service, could just be heard from the Lady Chapel altar.

Mrs Hitt had been sure Ewart Jones could fend for himself – as he had done. He had proved himself the boisterous, openhearted, un-secretive extrovert – not just the innocent at large some people had believed. The strength of his defence had ultimately lain in his openness. The same capacity for self or even mutual protection hadn't applied to Gerald Twist and Laura Purse – which was why Mrs Hitt had volunteered support for the mistiming of their alibi. She had even been prepared to make herself vulnerable in that particular cause. Poor Gerard. She smiled at the thought of his final unintentional blunder when he went to the hotel men's room after taking that telephone call. His disappearance had momentarily bothered Mark Treasure deeply.

'. . . *give us grace that we may cast away the works of darkness, and put upon us the armour of light, now in the time of this mortal life* . . .' The poetry of the Advent collect being recited at the altar seemed especially apposite. The candle was burning brightly.

Steering Jennifer Bliter away from dark works had been irritating and time-consuming. But it really wouldn't have done for her formally to have put Donald Welt under suspicion. The same had applied to Welt's own allegation about his being stalked nightly by a predatory Olive Merit. Happily Gilbert Hitt had stopped that calumny before its implications had burgeoned.

Of course, if the Dean had confided to his wife his belief that Cindy Larks had been with Pounder it would have created another target for her protection. But he hadn't told her – any more than she had told him about her even more circumstantial and uncharitable theory concerning Nutkin.

'. . . *and make your humble confession to Almighty God* . . .'

She listened while Canon Jones abjured his congregation to unburden their sins. Thank heaven the cathedral would stick to the old Book of Common Prayer so long as Gilbert was Dean. She didn't at all care for the uninspired language of the modern alternative book.

'Our authorised version's safe, I think. Public confessions won't be necessary,' said Treasure appropriately and in a half-whisper. He had just come in and settled in the chair beside Mrs Hitt.

'Well done.' She smiled back. 'Gilbert's satisfied?'

'Content, I should say.'

'That'll be enough. And you've settled Mr Pride the policeman, of course.' There was no questioning in the tone of this viscount's daughter whose ancestors had been making and breaking laws – and the keepers of laws – with total impunity through countless centuries, including a good deal of this one. For her it followed that a mercantile princeling as distinguished as Treasure would have had no difficulty directing a detective chief inspector into the right way of thinking.

'It must have been a great deal of trouble,' he said unexpectedly as both their gazes went automatically to centre on the candle she had lit: it was very close to burning out but there was enough of it left for the colour to distinguish it as special.

'Not much trouble really,' she replied softly. 'You learn all kinds of useful things at Mother's Union lectures. Making candles came up during the last miners' strike. It's quite simple. You have to remember to keep the wick twisted. That sealing wax melted to a very dark colour. I mixed in some white wax to make bulk. Appropriate it ended up as nearly purple, close to the church's seasonal colour for Advent.'

'In fact if the police had got hold of the wax I don't believe it would have damaged our cause.'

'After I'd risked my reputation by going secretly to a man's bedroom to take it?' She turned to him smiling.

'Very well. But you could have thrown it in the river instead of . . .'

'Oh, no, my dear.' She put a hand on his. 'That wouldn't have been nearly so final. So absolutely certain.'

'You don't trust the scientists? You think carbon tests could be wrong?'

'On the contrary, that they could be right.' She turned her eyes again to watch the flickering flame. 'Look at our relic expiring with dignity. A symbol, don't you think? And in the symbolic Presence. Up there in the chapel. The light of the flesh will soon go out, but the old stones stay. To comfort generations to come. Remember our bit of John Betjeman?'

The banker nodded agreement. And he dismissed lingering misgiving as the words of Ewart Jones floated back from the altar:

'. . . And although we be unworthy, through our manifold sins, to offer unto Thee any sacrifice, yet we beseech Thee to accept this . . .'

CRIMINALLY GOOD FICTION

Ranging from Golden Age mysteries and short stories, to thrillers, cosy crime and detective fiction, Bello's extensive crime list includes two founding members of the Crime Writers' Association, Andrew Garve and Josephine Bell; the early novels of popular children's author Nina Bawden; the creator of the 'inverted mystery', Roy Vickers; and one of the most popular crime authors writing today, Ann Cleeves.

# BELL◎

panmacmillan.com/bello

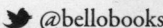 @bellobooks  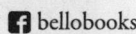 bellobooks

# PAN HERITAGE CLASSICS

Bringing wonderful classic books to a new audience.

MURDER AT
THE OLD VICARAGE
A CHRISTMAS MYSTERY
JILL McGOWN

THE HILLS
IS LONELY
LILLIAN BECKWITH

THE GROVE
OF EAGLES
A NOVEL OF ELIZABETHAN ENGLAND
WINSTON GRAHAM

A
LITTLE LOCAL
MURDER
ROBERT BARNARD

THE
CASE OF THE
MISSING BRONTE
ROBERT BARNARD

MARRYING
OFF MOTHER
AND OTHER STORIES
GERALD DURRELL

THE
ENCHANTED
PLACES
CHRISTOPHER
MILNE

MURDER IN
ADVENT
DAVID WILLIAMS

DR FINLAY'S
CASEBOOK
A J CRONIN